CRYPTID KINGDOM

CRYPTID ZOO BOOK 6

GERRY GRIFFITHS

SEVERED PRESS
HOBART TASMANIA

CRYPTID KINGDOM

DEDICATION

This is for Dr. Steve Amaro DVM

and the fabulous staff at Evergreen Veterinary Clinic

ALSO BY GERRY GRIFFITHS

DEATH CRAWLERS SERIES

DEATH CRAWLERS (BOOK 1)
DEEP IN THE JUNGLE (BOOK 2)
THE NEXT WORLD (BOOK 3)
BATTLEGROUND EARTH (BOOK 4)

CRYPTID ZOO SERIES

CRYPTID ZOO (BOOK 1)
CRYPTID COUNTRY (BOOK 2)
CRYPTID ISLAND (BOOK 3)
CRYPTID CIRCUS (BOOK 4)
CRYPTID NATION (BOOK 5)

STAND-ALONE NOVELS

SILURID
THE BEASTS OF STONECLAD MOUNTAIN
DOWN FROM BEAST MOUNTAIN
TERROR MOUNTAIN

1

MULCH

Standing under his umbrella in the shadowy alleyway, Dr. Haun Zhang watched the diners through the windows in the crowded restaurant across the street. Normally he would have chosen the bustling market place with its multiple points of entry and escape routes but a late-afternoon torrential rain had deterred people from shopping and forced the merchants to close down their stands early.

Wearing a prosthetic nose, a thin glue-on mustache, and horn-rimmed glasses, Zhang crossed the busy street, narrowly avoiding being struck by a passing yellow taxi and scurried onto the opposite sidewalk. Huddled under the eave in front of the restaurant, he closed his umbrella, shook off the rainwater, and stepped inside.

A woman in a blue hat and uniform greeted him and asked that he follow her into a huge dining room with round tables occupied by large groups of people. Food platters were heaped onto bamboo turntables so each person could rotate the server and fill their plates with various dishes.

The worker directed Zhang to an available chair at a table with eight young people who were already eating. As it was a sit-down buffet and the food was to be shared by everyone at the table, Zhang ordered plates of beef broccoli, eggplant, and two carved roasted ducks.

A couple sitting to his left overheard his generous order and gave him appreciative smiles. He grinned back but didn't say anything.

He took a serving spoon and filled the bowl in front of him with steamed rice.

Before he could remove his chopsticks from the wrapper, the man seated to his right put a chicken wing in Zhang's bowl. Realizing that the gracious man was probably the one paying for the others, Zhang accepted his hospitality and bowed his head.

For the next twenty minutes, Zhang enjoyed the selections, which included a spicy bowl of sliced ginger and spring onion soup, honey walnut prawns, and bok choy.

Everyone ate heartedly with their mouths open and smacked their lips.

Leaning back in his chair, a young man in a *Star Wars* T-shirt lit up a cigarette from across the table and blew smoke upward at the ceiling.

Zhang learned during their meal that the young man to his right was a student at university and was considering a sabbatical so he could travel with a group of friends. His name was Rong Tran but he was Westernized and liked to go by 'Joey' as he was a big fan of *Friends* and thought he looked like the actor Matt LeBlanc who played Joey Tribbiani on the popular TV show.

Even though the doctor didn't see the resemblance, he was taken by the young man's good looks. Joey's black hair was short-cropped and spiky. His eyes were black marbles and elliptical. He had an oval-shaped face, wide cheekbones, and a small nose.

He would be a perfect addition.

After most of the empty platters had been cleared from the turntable, a worker came with a serving tray of coffees. A few of the people at the table poured cream into their cups as the brewed blend was very strong and molasses-thick.

Zhang drank his black. He whispered to Joey that he would be honored to pay for the entire bill and the young man agreed.

Soon it was time for the young people to leave. Everyone stood and gave each other hugs before filing out between the tables.

Zhang paid 400 yauns at the cashier. He asked Joey if he had further plans for the evening. Joey wasn't sure. Perhaps he would be interested in going to the bar in the next room and having a drink.

Joey said yes and told his friends he would catch up to them later. He followed Zhang to the bar where they sat on red stools at the counter.

Joey ordered a Mango Martini; Zhang a Singapore Sling.

After four rounds of drinks discussing civil rights disparagement within the country, Joey excused himself and slipped off his stool, stumbling to the restroom.

While Joey was away, Zhang made sure no one was watching and emptied a small envelope of Vecuronium bromide into Joey's martini. Zhang picked up the stem glass and swirled the cocktail so the crystalline particles dissolved.

He knew he had only five minutes once the neuromuscular-blocking drug was ingested and it took effect.

So when Joey returned and sat on his stool, Zhang lied that he needed to get home to his family and insisted they drink up.

Joey looked disappointed and gulped down his martini in two swallows.

Once outside, Zhang opened his umbrella for the two of them as it was still raining. He continued their conversation from the bar to engage Joey while they crossed the street. Zhang had to hold up the inebriated young man when he stumbled onto the curb.

Insisting he knew a shortcut, Zhang led Joey into the alleyway, where his vehicle was parked. When Joey complained he was having trouble breathing and his muscles began to lock up, the doctor leaned him against the back bumper of his car and opened the trunk. Zhang was able to lift the gasping man into the trunk, fold up his legs, and shut the lid.

The twenty-seven-kilometer drive took Zhang 45 minutes. He pulled up to the twenty-foot wide solid metal security gate cantilevered in the stonewall that stretched upward of 30 feet. He pushed the button on a remote in the sedan's console and waited for the hinged barrier to swing open. He drove in and the gate closed behind him.

Driving between strings of lights on the ground resembling an airport landing strip, Zhang turned down a ramp into an underground parking lot. He saw about thirty vehicles, some privately owned, the others used by the employees.

Zhang pulled up in the stall behind a wide column marked with diagonal yellow and black stripes so motorists wouldn't crash into it. An electric cart with a cargo cover was parked in the next stall. He had picked this particular spot, as the armature on the closest surveillance camera was unable to point the lens in the direction of the parking spaces.

He got out of the car and popped the trunk. He stepped to the rear of the electric cart and opened the rear door. By then, Joey's body had turned into an awkward stiff bundle, making it difficult for Zhang to carry. After stuffing the still breathing young man into the electric cart's cargo hold, Zhang closed the door and the car trunk.

Zhang got behind the wheel of the electric cart and stepped on the accelerator.

The cart's motor hummed as he sped down the brightly lit tunnel at a brisk 5 miles per hour. He soon entered a labyrinth of more tunnels branching off the main thoroughfare and kept going.

He spotted a few employees in tan uniforms working the graveyard shift and made sure to turn his head as he passed by so they wouldn't see his face, even though he doubted they would recognize him in his disguise.

He heard a commotion of loud squeals and glanced to his left at the massive caged-in area filled with more than a hundred Chinese bamboo rats: each rodent larger than a beaver with long buck teeth.

He went down a passage that led to the center of the underground structure.

Zhang approached a huge block of concrete in the shape of a cylinder and came to a stop. He turned around and backed the cart up to a metal door. He got out of the cart, walked up to the door, and slid a keycard—which only he possessed—into the reader mounted on the wall.

The door slid open, revealing a small room with a table, a chest-high glass window, and what looked like a laundry chute.

He opened the back of the cargo bed, pulled Joey out by the arms, and dragged him into the room. Zhang swiped the keycard on the reader inside the room and the door closed.

The young man could not protest as his vocal cords were paralyzed and could only stare as Zhang knelt and stripped him naked.

The doctor took Joey's clothes and folded them neatly on the table. He placed the shoes on top. He took a moment and glanced through Joey's billfold but didn't remove anything. He put the wallet back in Joey's pants pocket.

Reaching under the table, he pulled a heavy-duty burn bag out of a cardboard box. He slipped the stack of garments and the pair of shoes inside, pulled the protective strip off the adhesive, and permanently sealed the bag.

He walked over and lowered the mouth of the chute. Lifting Joey up in his arms, Zhang stepped over and dropped the naked man down the metal duct. He could hear the thud on the other side of the wall.

Zhang looked through the window. The silo-shaped room was filled to the ceiling with rich, organic soil tapering off against the wall. He could see Joey lying on the dirt floor.

It took only a few seconds for the first tentacle to poke out of the loam, and like an eyeless thing, it began to feel its way along the floor.

A second root slithered out, followed by another.

They moved like a trio of serpents and wrapped around Joey's ankles.

The roots retreated slowly, pulling Joey's feet into the compost, then his legs, and continued to draw the still breathing man into the dirt until his entire body was gone.

Zhang grabbed the sealed burn bag from the table and left the room. He climbed into the electric cart and drove to another underground section.

Again, he used his keycard and gained access to the incinerator room.

Four laundry-style carts were parked against the wall, all completely filled with burn bags and sealed plastic pouches tagged with red hazardous waste stickers waiting to be incinerated.

Zhang dug down to the middle of the bags in the cart closest to the furnace and hid the burn bag with Joey's belongings.

Leaving the room and closing the door behind him, he hopped back in the electric cart.

He drove down the passageway to his subterranean living quarters where he planned to curl up on his bunk for a good night's sleep, unencumbered at having sacrificed the young student.

2

STONEWALLED

As they came down the mountain road, Nora Howard caught glimpses of Rocklin Falls through the windshield with every turn, the prominent church steeple at first and then gradually the slanted rooftops of the small rural town.

She glanced over at Jack Tremens who was behind the wheel. "You know, we could have just called."

"And stay cooped up in the house on such a beautiful day? I don't think so," Jack replied as he navigated another tight bend in the road.

"Have I been that bad?"

Jack shot her a quick glance. "I know it hasn't been easy the past three weeks." He turned his attention back to the road. "But something is bound to break."

"I wish I could believe that."

"Trust me. It will. He'll show up."

Reaching town, Jack headed down the main street and parked diagonally at the curb. They got out of the Ford Expedition and walked up to a glass door.

Sheriff Abraham "Abe" Stone was standing outside his office waiting to greet them as they came in. "Thought I saw you two pull up."

"Morning, Sheriff," Jack said.

"Any news?" Nora asked.

"Well..." Abe let the word drag out. "Nothing so far but I have some promising contacts," Abe said. "Care for some coffee?"

"Uh, no thanks," Jack replied. Nora declined with a headshake.

Abe stared down at the mug in his hand. "Can't say I blame you." He placed his half-filled mug on the counter.

"So no luck from the airports?" Nora asked.

"Nope. Airport security has been instructed to search all freight planes leaving the state but so far nothing."

"What about the shipping docks?" Jack asked.

"I've notified the Port Authority though they said it would be like finding a ping pong ball on Mt. Everest."

"In other words they wouldn't help."

"You have to realize the amount of freight that goes out of these ports is staggering," Abe said. "Oakland alone ships over 9 million cargo containers a year not to mention the other 10 major ports in California."

"Who says he wasn't transported across the country?" Jack said.

"Which would make that analogy more like finding a grain of rice in the Artic."

"What about Border Patrol?" Nora asked.

Abe shook his head.

"Certainly you've heard something from the FBI?"

"I have. A Special Agent Jennings."

"That name sounds familiar," Jack said. He looked over at Nora. "Wasn't he the lead investigator at Cryptid Zoo?"

"I think so," Nora replied and turned to the sheriff. "So what did Jennings have to say?"

"That he would look into it but he couldn't promise anything. To tell you the truth he didn't sound very optimistic."

"Unbelievable!" Nora shouted. "It's kidnapping for Christ sakes!"

"Technically, it's not," Abe said. "Lennie's not a person. His abduction is considered grand theft, and that is only if he has a state-issued license, which he doesn't. You know what would have helped?"

"What's that?" Jack asked.

"If they had passed that ridiculous bill putting all cryptids on the Endangered Species List. That would have made it a federal crime and the FBI would be all over it."

"That's crazy," Jack said.

Nora turned and gazed at the bulletin board outside Abe's office. She walked over and examined the photograph of her and her twelve-foot tall pet taken in front of the jungle foliage inside Cryptid Zoo's Biped Habitat. She was wearing her white lab coat and looked so small beside the giant Yeren covered in orange hair with a black skinned face and chest.

She placed a finger on the picture. "Lenny, where in the world are you?"

3

THE ARK

Lyle Mason stepped into the ship's galley. Being it was their last day onboard, he figured he would skip breakfast and poured himself a cup of coffee from the large urn at the end of the serving counter. He glanced around at the empty tables then spotted Todd Ramsey seated in the corner. Ramsey always reminded Mason of Mick Hucknall, the lead singer of the British pop band Simply Red, as he had a mop head of unruly red hair. He went over and sat down at his table.

"How's the S.O.S.?" Mason asked noticing the half-eaten plate of creamed chipped beef on Ramsey's tray.

Ramsey gave a disgusted look and shook his head. "Bland as hell." He pushed the tray to the center of the table.

"They don't call it shit on a shingle for nothing," Mason said. He took a sip of his coffee and made a face. "Tastes like panther piss."

"I wouldn't know," Ramsey said.

Mason parked his cup on Ramsey's tray.

"If I didn't know any better, I'd swear they were trying to poison us."

"Just be glad to be back on dry land," Mason said.

"Well, we're not exactly there yet." Ramsey grabbed his tray and stood up from the table. Mason got up and waited by the door while Ramsey slid his tray into the small scullery window for the dishwasher.

They went out together down a narrow passageway to a hatchway that led to the outside deck running alongside the ship's bridge. Mason put on his sunglasses to shield his eyes from the bright late-morning sun. He could hear the high-pitch caw of the seagulls circling above the antennas and radar masts.

Mason and Ramsey leaned on the railing and took in the panoramic view of the busy shipping port from the upper deck of the livestock carrier, five stories above the wharf.

Two container ships, each as long as three football fields, were being loaded in the far berths with orange, red, blue, and green 20-foot long sea vans which looked like giant Rubik's cubes stacked on the decks. Twenty-five story harbor cranes towered over the loading docks like alien space invaders.

Looking down the side of the ship, Mason saw that two sets of ramps had been deployed. The narrow ramp nearer the stern was being used to offload cattle single file from the ship onto the waiting semi truck trailers, a tedious process, as there were over 3,000 steers onboard. The ramp closer to the bow was wider with pedestrian walkways on each side so the handlers could prod the sheep along: all 14,000.

It was going to be a long day.

"Can't believe we've been stuck on this barge for three weeks," Ramsey said.

"Now you know why they call it a slow boat to China."

Ramsey glanced at Mason's left arm as he had his denim sleeves rolled up. "Man, that looks bad."

Mason looked at his scarred arm. Forty-five stitches and it looked like a jigsaw puzzle. It was a miracle it was still attached to his shoulder. He raised his hand, managing to flex his fingers, and felt the tendon pull tight up through his forearm. "Good as new," he muttered.

They entered a hatchway and walked by rows of ventilation turbines used to exhaust the ammonia and foul smell of the animal feces from the lower levels.

Going down the steel stairwell, Mason thought it strange seeing the pens empty, when only yesterday, they were so crowded with sheep, the tightly-knit mass looked like a shaggy wool carpet. Mason followed Ramsey down the stairs until they reached the bottom level and the enclosed stockades.

"You think we'll have them all sedated by nightfall?" Ramsey asked.

"I hope so," Mason replied. He could hear the six Xing-Xings screeching and racing about the huge cage. They always seemed to have endless energy and were in constant motion. He gazed through the bars at the fifty-pound primates that resembled brown-face baboons. When it came time for transporting, they would have to take extra precautions making sure the creatures were knocked out, as they were extremely dangerous.

But then, so was every creature on this level.

Mason and Ramsey continued walking down the aisle between the stockades.

To their right, were the four *Alxasaurus*. The dinosaurs were as tall as ostriches with long necks and tails. Their entire bodies were covered with aquamarine colored feathers. Instead of wings, they had short arms with large-fingered claws.

On the left, a dozen turkey-sized *Caudipeteryx* gathered together in the middle of their enclosure. They were more flamboyant with dark blue feathers and red-tipped plumage on the tips of their wings and tails. They, too, had long clawed fingers.

Mason could hear the other creatures, restless in their enclosures. Maybe they sensed that the ship was no longer in motion and were anxious at what might come next.

He walked up and peered through the bars of the last cage. The creature inside sat on the floor like a giant toddler. "Hey there, big guy. It won't be long now."

For the past three weeks, Mason had been the only one that interacted with the creature and they had formed somewhat of a bond, though Mason knew to be wary. At one thousand pounds and twelve feet tall, the giant Yeren—the Chinese version of the Pacific Northwest Bigfoot—was certainly a far cry from a domestic pet though it did have a given name.

Mason went over to the food sacks and grabbed an open fifty-pound bag of potatoes. He reached in and began tossing the rustic spuds into the cage. The Yeren responded by scooting across the floor and snatching up each potato and stuffing it into his mouth. Soon his cheeks bulged so full, drool oozed out of the corners of his mouth.

"Guess you won't be wanting gravy with that, eh Lenny?" Mason said with a laugh.

4

AMY'S BIG SURPRISE

Caroline Rollins got into the mindset to confront the man with the knife, standing only five feet away. He was big, athletic, and outweighed her by seventy pounds. He held the blade firmly in his right hand with the tip pointed directly at her chest and looked as though he had done this kind of thing before. His face showed no emotion, eyes fixed on her like a calculating predator sizing up his kill, waiting for the perfect moment to strike.

She made a slight sidestep with her left foot. He countered by staying in front of her, blocking her path and giving her no way to escape. He was close enough that if she turned to run, he would be on her in a flash.

There was no point in yelling for help. She was on her own. It was either fight or flight and she had already made the decision that to flee would be suicide.

Caroline never took her eyes off the menacing blade. One quick jab and it could all be over.

The man lunged.

Caroline caught a quick whiff of his sweat, the body odor masked by cheap cologne. She grabbed the wrist of his knife hand with her left hand and then clamped it like a tight-fitting manacle with her other hand. She twisted his arm in an unnatural position, which threw him off balance, giving her the opportunity to deliver a sidekick to his groin. As he went down, she struck his knuckles with the heel of her hand. His fingers immediately opened up and he dropped the knife. She kicked at him again, this time in the ribs and then in the head.

She retrieved the knife and pretended to run.

"Excellent," praised Sensei James Carson.

Amy Chen, and five other karate students stood around the edge of the blue gymnasium mat. Everyone was barefoot and wore white gi jackets and loose-fitting pants with sash belts tied around their waists. Two students wore yellow belts, the other three green. Amy's belt was brown.

Gabe Wells—the defeated knife-wielding attacker—wore the same attire and had a brown belt. He quickly sprang from the mat onto his feet. He faced Caroline, who also wore a brown belt. They both bowed to one another.

Sensei Carson, Master Black Belt and owner of Dragon Claw Dojo located a few blocks from the university, taught martial arts to dedicated students as well as women's self-defense classes to those wanting to be able to protect themselves on and off campus. He held out his hand.

Caroline gave him the rubber knife and bowed to her instructor. He returned the bow and looked at the class. "Number one thing to always remember when defending against a knife attack: always stay out of the path of the knife. If you don't, more times than not, you will end up being stabbed. Once you have deflected the initial attack, then you can counter with a crippling blow to the head or body."

He turned to Gabe. "Nice job, Gabe."

"Thank you, Sensei," Gabe replied.

"That's our session for today," Sensei Carson said.

The students bowed to the sensei, ending the class.

"You two looked really intense out there," Amy said to Gabe and Caroline as they crossed the room to retrieve their karate gear bags.

"Maybe a little too intense," Gabe said, rubbing his inner thigh. He glanced over at Caroline. "Next time, watch the groin shot."

"Oh, I'm sorry, a little too close for comfort?" Caroline said with a wink.

"Laugh all you want."

"Better watch out, next time I might not pull my kicks."

"You're the one that'll suffer later, not me."

"Amy, are you hearing this?" Caroline said to her friend as the three of them slipped on their sandals. The other students had already filed out the front door and Sensei Carson had gone to his office in the back.

"Guys, behave," Amy said. "I have something to tell you."

"What's that?" Caroline asked, rummaging through her tote bag to make sure she had her headgear, boxing gloves, chest and foot protectors for sparring, along with her two trident sai swords.

"Remember I told you my father works at a travel agency?"

"Yeah, so?" Gabe said.

"He was able to get us tickets very cheap."

"What are you saying, Amy? You went and had your dad buy us plane tickets and didn't consult us first?"

"I wanted it to be a big surprise for spring break."

"Wait a second," Gabe said. "I was thinking of asking Caroline if she wanted to go visit my parents during spring break."

Caroline turned to Gabe. "You were?"

"Yeah."

"Guys, you can't pass this up," Amy said.

"Why not?" Caroline said.

"It's a real good deal. And my father said he would pay for it."

"Then you better tell him to get his money back," Gabe said. "I don't think we can go."

"There's a problem," Amy said.

"Yeah? What's that?"

"There's no refund."

"Seriously, Amy?" Caroline said. "So if we don't go, your father can't get his money back?"

"Maybe you could get someone else to go with you," Gabe said.

"Guys! I want you to go!"

"But what if we don't have the money right now?" Caroline said.

"No worries. You don't have to pay him back. His way of showing his appreciation for you being my friends and helping me with school. To not go would hurt his feelings."

"Amy, I can't believe you did this." Caroline looked at Gabe. He didn't say anything and shrugged his shoulders.

"You have passports, right?" Amy asked.

"Yes, of course. Why? Where are we going?"

"To where I grew up as a little girl."

"What?" Gabe said. "Your father booked us a flight to China?"

"This gets crazier by the minute. Where would we stay?" Caroline asked.

"Don't worry," Amy said with a big grin. "It's all been arranged. We can stay with my cousin for free. He'll feed us and everything."

Gabe looked at Caroline. "Well, what do you think?"

"Could be fun. What about your parents?"

"We can see them another time. But I better let them know of our plans. What about yours?"

"Being a senator's daughter, my dad's always busy and we haven't gotten to travel much. I'm sure they won't object." Caroline turned and smiled at Amy. "So, when do we leave?"

"Three days."

5

NIGHT CONVOY

Mason held onto the handgrip like it might actually save his life in the event of a crash as they took yet another high-speed turn on the perilous shoreline road. It was dark upon leaving the harbor but there was enough moonlight shimmering on the ocean that he could see the white-capped waves crashing on the boulders at the base of the 500-foot precipice every time they got too close to the shoulder as there were no guardrails to obscure his view.

He glanced at the side-view mirror and saw the headlights of the small convoy of trucks barreling behind them, weaving around each bend.

Ramsey sat in the middle between Mason and the Chinese driver.

"You know, it wouldn't hurt to slow down," Ramsey said to the driver. The man ignored him and kept staring straight ahead, both hands on the wheel, cigarette dangling out of his mouth. Maybe he was deaf or didn't understand English.

Mason suspected it might be both.

"Mind cracking open your window," Ramsey said, fanning the smoke from his face. Again, the man was mute like he hadn't heard the request.

Mason figured rather than keep nagging the man it was easier for him to open his own window. He pushed the button on the armrest and lowered the glass halfway down.

The cross draft drew more smoke into Ramsey's face.

"Jesus, give me a break," Ramsey bitched.

Mason raised his window.

The driver snubbed his butt into the overfilled dashboard ashtray and left it smoldering. Ramsey reached over and put it out just as the compulsive-smoker lit up another cigarette.

The road reached a summit and turned inland, giving Mason and Ramsey their first glimpse of the sprawling metropolis of Hangshong Province.

"Wow, will you look at that," Ramsey said.

The city was aglitter with futuristic-looking high-rises and stunning glass spires and looked like a picture-perfect postcard.

"A guy on the ship said this is one of China's wealthiest cities," Mason said.

"Looks pretty big," Ramsey said.

"Yeah, over two million people."

Instead of heading straight into the city, the driver veered off the highway and onto a two-lane road that took them out into the country through vast partials of paddy fields and more open land. They continued on for about twenty minutes.

"What the hell is that? A prison?" Ramsey said.

"Looks like a fortress," Mason said, once he saw the thirty–foot tall wall lit up by spotlights shining up from the ground as if promoting a Hollywood premiere.

"Check that out," Ramsey said, pointing through the windshield.

Mason spotted guards looking down from the parapet walkway.

The driver drove alongside the sheer barrier until they reached a metal gate that was already opening. A fierce giant dragonhead with its mouth agape arched the entrance.

Mason glanced in his side-view mirror and saw the other trucks following behind as they entered the massive compound. Though it was dark, he could see eerie silhouettes of sharp-edged buildings and strange structures in the moonlight. Before he could register what he was seeing, the truck slowed and dipped down into an underground tunnel leading into a wide parking area with bored passageways branching in different directions.

The vehicles pulled up side-by-side and the engines turned off.

Mason opened his door and climbed down from the cab. Ramsey jumped out; both of them glad to finally be away from the driver's second-hand smoke.

As they walked to the rear of the truck, Mason saw an attractive Chinese woman in a tan shirt and pants, along with twenty Chinese men wearing similar uniforms standing behind her like a small platoon, some armed with four-foot long gaffs.

The woman stepped away from the group. She approached Mason and Ramsey and gave them each a bow. "Hello. I am Song Liu. I am here to assist you."

"Nice to meet you," Mason said. "I'm—"

"Lyle Mason," Song said, "And you are Todd Ramsey."

"That's right," Ramsey replied. "I don't think our driver understood a word we said to him on the way over here. Does this mean you'll be our interpreter?"

"Yes," Song said. "Like you, I also work with the animals."

"We should get them settled in before their sedatives wear off," Mason said.

"Very well." Song shouted to the drivers in Chinese and the men climbed back in their trucks. She turned to Mason. "Do you want to go with the raptors?"

"I don't think they'll be much trouble. Ramsey and I should stay with the primates." Mason watched Song flag the drivers in the two trucks carrying the bioengineered prehistoric birds. The engines started and the trucks drove off down a side tunnel.

"Come with me," Song said.

Mason and Ramsey followed the woman to an electric golf cart. Song got behind the wheel, Mason in the seat next to her. Ramsey sat in the rear bench seat.

The two remaining trucks started up and headed down an opposite tunnel. Song waited for the lingering exhaust fumes to dissipate then followed the trucks for a short distance to find the men already removing the heavy canvas tarps covering the cargo holds. The trucks had backed up to separate cages with open sliding doors and were butted up to the bars so there was no chance of an animal escaping.

Extending their gaffs into the cargo hold, the men began to prod the sleeping Xing-Xings. The 6 fifty-pound baboons stirred awake, not in the best of moods. They snarled and charged the bars, rattling the cage and screeching like a pack of hyenas.

The men seemed to enjoy tormenting the apes.

"Okay, okay. Back off," Ramsey said. The men ignored him as they didn't understand English.

A man got on the edge of the rear bumper and shoved his gaff between the bars to jab the closest Xing-Xing.

Even though the creature was half the weight of the man, it was three times as strong. The man overextended the gaff inside the cage; just enough for the ape to grab the man's forearm.

Mason heard the bone snap despite the ruckus.

"Get back!" Ramsey yelled. He grabbed a man standing at the side of the truck and pulled him away from the cage then dissuaded another man.

Song yelled for the men to stop. They turned to her and lowered their gaffs.

Mason jumped up on the rear bumper. He pounded on the bars. The ape released the man's oddly bent arm and vaulted out of the cargo hold into the containment. The other Xing-Xings shrieked and dashed from the back of the truck. Ramsey shut the sliding cage door, sealing the creatures inside.

The whimpering man was carried away.

"He's lucky he didn't get his arm ripped off," Ramsey said.

Mason noticed his friend give him an apologetic look.

He heard a fierce snarl and looked over his shoulder. A man stood by the next truck and was prodding the Yeren in the foot.

"I wouldn't do that," Mason shouted.

Song intervened, speaking harshly to the man. He gave her a curt bow and stepped away.

"It's all right, Lennie," Mason said. "No one is going to hurt you."

The Yeren narrowed his eyes at Mason like he didn't believe him and huffed.

Song stepped over to Mason and said, "I apologize for the men's rude behavior."

Mason grinned. "That's okay. I can be a little overprotective."

"I know. I, too, have bonded," Song said.

Mason heard a boisterous horselaugh, which he knew had to be Ramsey.

"When you two are through *bonding*," Ramsey said still laughing, "how about we get him tucked in? I'm talking about the Yeren of course. I don't know about you but I'm beat."

Mason saw Ramsey giving him a look that translated to: *That okay with you, Romeo?*

"Shut up," Mason said, even though Ramsey hadn't uttered a word.

Lennie was too groggy to put up much of a fuss and after a little coaxing, scooted off the flat bed of the truck, and into the high-ceiling cage tall enough that he could stand erect. He sat in a corner furthest from the front of the cage.

After Mason and Ramsey made sure there was adequate water and food provided for their wards, they got back into Song's electric cart. They went down the main tunnel past a section of clothier display windows, cafeteria-style eateries, banking ATM kiosks, and an arcade with pinball machines and video games.

"Everything you need is down here," Song said.

"It's like an underground city." Mason was rather impressed.

The hum of the electric cart whined down and Song stopped in front of a closed metal door. She climbed out of the cart and swiped a keycard in the reader on the wall, which slid open the door. "Let me show you where you'll stay."

Mason and Ramsey accompanied her down a long hallway with a series of private billets. "Here are your living quarters," Song said, using a different keycard to open the door. She handed the access card to Mason and gave Ramsey one as well.

Recessed lighting in the ceiling automatically came on illuminating the spacious room. Oriental tapestries ordained one wall by the sitting area consisting of two rattan chairs and a low back couch set around a long short-legged maple coffee table.

The separate sleeping quarters—partially screened off by a room divider painted with falling leaves and a flock of swallows in flight—had two twin birch framed beds that were mere inches off the laminate wood plank flooring and matching nightstands with tiger designs on the porcelain lamps with white linen shades.

It lacked a fully functional kitchen but had a mini refrigerator. A bowl of mixed fruit was on an oval table tucked against the wall with three stiff back chairs.

Mason saw their duffle bags and other gear had been brought into the room and was lined up by the room divider. He smiled at Song. "Thank you."

Song gave him a slight bow.

"When will we see you again?" Mason asked.

"Tomorrow. I will be here at eight o'clock sharp." Song backed out of the room and closed the door behind her.

Mason turned and saw Ramsey with an orange. His friend bit into the rind and began peeling the fruit with his thumb. He halved the orange and handed it to Mason.

Mason separated a wedge and stuffed it in his mouth. The mandarin orange was sweet and juicy. It was so good he popped in another segment.

Ramsey plopped down on a rattan chair, extended his legs onto the coffee table, and crossed his ankles with his heels on the surface. He finished his part of the orange and tossed the curled rind on the table. "Well, what do you think? Not too shabby, eh?"

Mason sat down on the low back couch. He reached over, slapped Ramsey's boots, and picked up the peeling. "Best to show some respect and not trash the place."

"Oh yeah. Sorry," Ramsey said and removed his feet from the table. "So what happens now?"

"I have no idea. I guess we play it one day at a time."

"Ever wonder what happened to the rest of the guys?"

"Who knows," Mason said.

"Think we'll ever see that wacko doctor again?"

"McCabe? I hope not. Guy scares the shit out of me."

"You and me both."

6

AIRSICK

Lucas Finder gazed out the cabin window at the knife-edged wing slicing through the clouds as the long-range Gulfstream G650ER cruised at a speed of 500 miles an hour over the Pacific Ocean.

Swiveling his chair around, Finder couldn't help admiring the plush interior. The fuselage had eight windows on each side and seating for 11 people with high-backed contoured seats with side tables, and two sprawling leather couches. A 55-inch flat screen was mounted on the bulkhead in the rear, not far from the lavatory.

The 75 million-dollar aircraft was the most expensive private jet on the market, which was only a drop in the bucket for Finder's multi-billionaire boss.

"What's wrong, Lucas?" Carter Wilde asked, occupying the vacant seat next to Finder. "You haven't touched your drink." Wilde had on a $50,000 finely tailored blue Kiton K-5 business suit which had taken 45 tailors 25 hours to stitch, a big contrast from the unimposing black cassock and black boots that Finder was used to seeing his boss wearing when the obscenely-rich man was going through his superior-than-God phase. He'd since lost the ponytail and his gray hair and beard were neatly trimmed.

Finder stared down at the tumbler of Beluga Epicure vodka that ran about $10,000 a bottle. "Sorry, sir. My stomach is still in a knot," he lied, inferring he was still queasy from the turbulence they had experienced half an hour ago.

"I've had bumpier rides on Mulholland Drive. Sure it isn't something else?" Wilde pressed.

As Chief Operating Officer of Wilde Enterprises, it was Finder's job to oversee Carter Wilde's conglomerate of businesses all over the world. It seemed lately his boss had his finger in just about every corporate pie. But not all of Wilde's ventures were proving fruitful. "We hit some setbacks," Finder confessed.

"Don't tell me. The Egyptians."

"After much negotiation, they passed. Didn't want another Cryptid Zoo fiasco."

"What about France?"

"There's too much going on with the riots and that stupid gasoline tax."

"So we're not breaking ground next to the Eiffel Tower?"

"No, sir."

"What about the others?"

"I'm still working on them."

"What a bunch of weasels," Wilde said, taking a sip of his 23-year-old bourbon whiskey.

"Well, at least the Chinese held up their part of the agreement," Finder said, knowing his boss was disappointed having learned there was no longer interest in Wilde's projects to fund and build Cryptid Zoo domes in two more foreign countries, making it now a total of four.

"That they did. Thanks to Henry."

Finder knew Wilde was referring to Henry Chang, the wealthiest man in China. "Don't forget his daughter, Luan. The woman's a genius."

"Who's a genius?" a voice said. It was Dr. Joel McCabe. He was dressed casual: blue blazer, yellow polo shirt, and black trousers. He sat down on the couch facing them and took a gulp of his Samuel Adams' Utopias.

"We were talking about Luan Chang," Wilde said.

"Oh, her. Whatever happened to Howard?" McCabe asked.

"Professor Nora Howard is no longer in my employment and hasn't been for some time. You know that."

"So what are you saying?" McCabe put his beer bottle down on a glass table. "That Luan Chang is a better bioengineer than Howard?"

"Possibly. We won't know until we see for ourselves."

"You think she's better than me?" McCabe leaned forward with his forearms on his thighs and gave Wilde a challenging glare.

"Like I said, we won't know until we see for ourselves."

"Screw you, Carter."

"I thought you might say that, Joel."

McCabe got up. "I need another beer."

Finder figured why not at $150 a bottle.

"Sometimes he can be such a pain," Wilde said.

Finder often questioned why his boss continued to associate with McCabe and keep him around after what the unhinged man had done, first creating an explosion under the original Cryptid Zoo dome and then unleashing a horde of vicious creatures to ruin the grand opening of Wilde Skyway which was to be the tallest building in the world until

Saudi Arabia announced it was building Jeddah Tower, a 824-foot taller skyscraper.

McCabe made his way up the aisle between the six men seated up front, two of them Wilde's personal bodyguards; the other four archaic members of Wilde's pro-cryptid activists group: the Cryptos. The doctor waltzed up to the flight attendant standing next to the liquor cart and gave her his empty bottle. She reached in the cooler and handed McCabe another beer.

"We're about to land," Finder heard Wilde say. "I'm counting on a good visit. I have a lot riding on this joint-venture."

"I know, sir."

Wilde patted Finder on the knee and returned up front.

Finder stared down at his glass. It didn't matter how many times it had been filtered or how smooth the vodka was going down, it would still feel like molten lava flowing through the knots in his stomach.

7

STAKEOUT

FBI Special Agent Anna Rivers's back was killing her from sitting so long and staring out the windshield. She grabbed the infrared night vision binoculars off the dashboard and focused in on the loading dock poorly lit up under a single floodlight on the other side of the chain-link fencing. She could make out the sign over the bay doors: WILDE FIREARMS—A DIVISION OF WILDE ENTERPRISES

It was going on four in the morning and they'd been parked back in the trees for almost seven hours waiting for something to happen.

"Did you know the average person will spend 10 years during their lifetime standing in line?" said her partner, Mack Hunter, slouched behind the steering wheel.

"I guess there are things worse than a stakeout," Anna said. She rubbed her right eye with her knuckles. "I'd give your left nut for some shuteye."

"Yeah, I bet you would," Mack replied.

Anna glanced over and saw her partner pull a worn paperback out of his jacket pocket. He opened the book and shined a penlight on the page. "Seriously, Mack. I don't think this is the time for reading."

"You like it when I read to you."

"Shut up. Better not be another one of your spy thrillers."

"No," Mack said. "It's an edition of *Guinness Book of World Records*."

"Oh, jeez."

"What, afraid you might learn something?"

Anna sighed and stared back out the windshield.

Mack studied the page with the penlight. "Did you know the longest recorded time a person has gone without sleep is 264 hours? Imagine staying awake for 11 days."

"Believe me, I can imagine." She put a hand up to her mouth to stifle a yawn.

He flipped through the pages. "Oh, here's a good one. Did you know the largest coffee cup holds over 6,000 gallons?"

"Like that would fit on my Keurig," Anna said.

An engine rumbling beyond the trees got their attention.

Mack switched off the penlight and tossed the book on the seat.

Anna gazed through the night vision goggles. She saw a rental truck pull up to the rear gate. The passenger door opened. "Someone's getting out," she said and watched a dark figure in a hooded sweatshirt jump down, walk up and unlock the gate, then climb back into the cab.

"Fancy that," Mack said. "Must have a key to the city."

The truck drove through, hung a U-turn, and backed up to the loading dock.

"Better make sure everyone's seeing this," Mack said. He pulled out his service pistol and laid the weapon on the car seat.

Anna clicked on her handheld radio. "Bravo, this is Alpha. We have visual."

"Roger, Alpha," replied a voice over the radio's speaker.

"Charlie, do you copy that?" Anna spoke into the radio.

"Roger, Alpha."

The same man that had opened the gate got out of the truck while the driver remained behind the wheel with the engine running. Coming around to the rear of the vehicle, the man bent down and raised the rollup door. Four men, wearing hoodies and dressed in black, exited the cargo hold.

Anna zoomed in hoping to identify them. Only their eyes could be seen in the balaclava masks, the lower facial portions resembling that of a cryptid creature, either a Thunderbird's beak or a Bigfoot's snarling mouth.

"Well?" Mack said. "Are they Wilde's radicals?"

"They're Cryptos all right."

Instead of breaking down the door with a battering ram to the Receiving area, one of the burglars used a keycard and swiped it down the reader. The door sprung open and the men rushed inside.

Anna handed Mack the portable radio. She drew her service weapon.

"On my mark," Mack spoke into the handheld radio.

In less than a minute the thieves came out, two men on each end carrying long wooden crates.

"NOW!" Mack shouted into the radio and jumped out of the unmarked sedan.

Anna threw open her door.

Two black SUVs came out of nowhere—sirens chirping with blue flashing lights pulsating on the grills—and sped toward the open gate.

One Ford Expedition blocked the gate while the other vehicle barreled up to the front of the idling truck.

Doors flung open and agents carrying handguns and riot shotguns piled out in bulletproof vests and blue FBI insignia blazers.

The driver of the truck hit the accelerator, plowed into the side of the FBI vehicle blocking it in, and tried to bulldoze its way through. Two agents aimed their weapons at the windshield and rapid-fired, punching twenty or more holes through the tempered glass. The bloody-faced man slumped over the steering wheel.

Anna and Mack raced through the trees on foot and dashed into the yard.

The men on the dock had crouched behind the crates and were returning fire with Uzi machinegun pistols. A heavy volley of bullets cut down an agent running to the side of the loading dock.

Hiding behind a tall stack of wooden pallets, Anna and Mack had a sideview of the Cryptos hunkered behind the wooden boxes of armament. They each took a shot and nailed two unsuspecting men but then one of them turned and unleashed a deadly barrage at Anna and Mack. They dove to the ground as the wooden pallets burst apart into splintery pieces and rained down on their heads like tornado debris.

A series of shotgun blasts could be heard along with some high-pitched screams.

Anna got to her feet and saw the agents swarming the loading dock. The Cryptos were all dead except for one, kneeling on the cement. Rather than surrender and be taken alive, the anarchist shoved the muzzle of his Uzi into his mouth and pulled the trigger.

The agents on the dock watched in horror as the back of the man's skull exploded in a gory mosaic mess on the wall behind him.

"Jesus," Mack said. "What is wrong with these people?"

"All clear," an agent called out to the others.

"Well, now we know. Carter Wilde is willfully supplying his Cryptos with firearms," Anna said. Her cell phone chimed in her pocket. She took it out and answered. She listened for a moment. "That's great news, Director. We'll be ready to go." She ended the call.

"What was that about?" Mack asked.

"Seems we have a lead."

"On what?"

"Carter Wilde. Let's finish up here and I'll fill you in on the drive back," Anna said as they walked over to assist the other agents.

8

IMPROMPTO TOUR

The next morning after Mason and Ramsey had eaten breakfast and tended to their cryptids, Song picked them up in her electric cart and took them topside for a tour.

Mason had no idea what to expect as they rode up the ramp and came out onto a stone paved path with lush garden settings on both sides. He glanced to his left and saw a tall wall that stretched beyond his line of vision along the tops of the bordering hedges and flowering cherry blossom trees. "So what's with the wall?" Mason asked.

"You don't recognize it?" Song asked. She stopped the cart. She looked at Mason sitting next to her then glanced over her shoulder at Ramsey seated behind Mason.

Both men shook their heads.

"It is a replica of the Great Wall of China," Song said.

"Yeah, but that's over a thousand miles long," Ramsey said.

"Thirteen thousand miles to be exact," Song said. "No, the wall you see only surrounds the Kingdom which is 100 acres."

"Kingdom?" Mason asked.

"Yes, Cryptid Kingdom."

"Never heard of it," Ramsey said.

"Me neither," Mason said.

"That is because we don't open for another two days."

"So those creatures we brought are going to be exhibits?"

"They are only a few." Song stepped on the accelerator and the electric cart hummed down the paved trailway.

As they rode down the narrow strip, Mason spotted groundskeepers and maintenance people working various tasks. Mason craned his head back and looked up at the underside of a steel roller coaster suspended off the ground, running parallel twenty feet away from the thirty-foot tall wall.

Song noticed him gazing up. "That is Cobra Fury. It goes around the entire grounds. It has eight corkscrew turns like a serpent."

"So what is this, some kind of amusement park?" Ramsey said.

"Oh, much more." Song drove over an arched bridge spanning a bubbling brook surrounded by greenery and artificial boulders used to conceal pumps and machinery.

Mason saw an ornate structure with orange tiles on three tiered swooping roofs. A series of orange cement steps led up to an archway. "What is that place?" he asked.

"That is Yeren Temple where your Yeren will be. It is a high honor."

"I'd like to take a look inside."

"You will. Later," Song said and kept driving.

The next building was circular in design and had blue tile roofs.

"What are those things in front?" Ramsey asked, leaning forward in the back seat.

Mason saw two giant bronze statues like bookends bordering the front steps. The bigheaded beasts had round balls on their manes, broad shoulders, and sat on their haunches. Armor plates covered their front legs. Their sharp claws seemed to dig into the cement.

"They are the loyal guardians of Fu Lion Pavilion."

"So what are they guarding?" Ramsey asked.

"Fu Lions of course."

"What?" Mason said.

"Up ahead is the Birdhouse."

Mason spotted a white two-story building with a pavilion roof. Wraparound decks with waist-high fences surrounded the structure on both floors so that people could walk around the aviary and peer through the six-foot diameter glass portals at the exhibits inside. It looked like a giant decorative birdhouse one would expect to see perched on top of a post in someone's backyard.

As they reached a corner of the oblong property, Song steered right for about 100 feet and stopped the cart. "If you look up, you will see Sky-High."

Mason stared up at the chairlifts that stretched to the other side of the grounds and continued back for a full loop around the center of the park.

Part way down he spotted a circular area the size of four backyard swimming pools butted together, cordoned off with fifteen-foot tall chain-link fencing rimmed with razor wire. "What's that for?" he asked.

"The Wuhnan Toads," Song said.

"All that for a bunch of frogs," Ramsey said.

"What about that?" Mason said, pointing to a ladder just outside the fence, leading up to a small platform overhanging the enclosure.

"That is how we feed them."

Mason looked back at his friend. Ramsey gave him a shrug.

Instead of driving the entire inside perimeter, Song chose to take a shortcut beneath the Sky-High chairlifts. To their left was a gigantic water park with a body of water for a wave machine and four tube slides emptying into a large lagoon and what appeared to be the glass front to a giant aquarium.

A strange looking tree with widespread branches and hanging fruit stood in a stonewall planter in the middle of the grounds like a giant centerpiece.

"That's odd looking," Mason said. "What kind of tree is that?"

"It's called Jinmenju, the human-face tree. Sometimes at night you can hear the fruit laughing."

"Okay," Ramsey said skeptically from the backseat.

Song turned the electric cart and gave the tree a wide berth. "There is much more to see but we should get to work."

Mason was fine with that. He wanted to see how Lennie was acclimating to his new surroundings.

On their way back to the tunnel entrance, Mason spotted a small group of people and a news crew setting up near Yeren Temple.

9

NEWS UPDATE

News reporter Jenny Lee checked her notes, tossed back her shoulder-length hair, and held her microphone up to her face. "I'm ready, Jim." She waited for the red light to appear on the bulky video camera. "This is Jenny Lee, reporting live from Hangshong Province, China. Today we have been given an exclusive look inside the most anticipated theme park in the world—Cryptid Kingdom, which is due to open in two days. With me is renowned Chinese cryptozoologist, Dr. Luan Chang."

Jim moved the camera to include the scientist in the frame. Luan wore her hair back in a tight bun and looked studious in her large frame glasses and white lab coat.

"So Dr. Chang, please tell our viewers what guests should expect when they visit Cryptid Kingdom."

"Well, we have a world-class water park, and I've been told, one of the most thrilling roller coaster rides on the continent."

"Have you ridden the roller coaster?" Jenny asked.

"No, it is much too scary for me," Luan said, feigning a frightened expression.

"Tell us about your work."

"Our team of scientists and myself have successfully created and brought to life mythical creatures from our cultural heritage."

"But don't you need DNA in order to do that?"

"Yes, that is correct."

"But if these creatures are only legends," Jenny said, "and never existed, how is that possible?"

"By writing new biological instructions and creating new bonds of double-stranded DNA. We had a general idea how they should look, their behavioral patterns, and went from there."

"You make it sound so simple," Jenny said.

"We have been working on this project for more than ten years. Believe me, it was far from simple."

"I guess you have plenty of support from your father."

"Yes, it is true. As you probably already know, my father not only funded our research, he is also the major owner of Cryptid Kingdom along with a silent partner."

"I understand Dr. Haun Zhang is part of your team?"

Luan paused then said, "That is correct. As you can imagine, creating these creatures has been a monumental task."

"But after what he did, I would think—"

Luan interrupted the reporter by saying, "Dr. Zhang was never convicted."

"Some say your father was influential in Dr. Zhang's acquittal."

"Perhaps you would like to see one of our exhibits," Luan said, deftly changing the subject.

"But of course. That *is* why we are here," Jenny said.

The news team followed Luan down a cobblestone path bordered by rows of cherry blossom trees. They reached the front steps to a structure that looked like it had been constructed centuries ago by a past dynasty. The orange tiled roofs bowed in the middle and swept upward at the tips in perfect symmetry.

Jenny followed Luan as they stepped through the arched entrance.

Jim turned the light on his video camera even though there was ample sunlight filtering down from the overhead skywell into the massive room with ordain columns and marble flooring.

"So where are we exactly?" Jenny asked, holding her microphone out for Luan to speak into.

"This is Yeren Temple," Luan said.

Jenny turned slowly to gaze about the room. She froze when she saw a huge creature standing behind a thick-paned glass enclosure. "Oh my God," she gasped. "Jim, are you getting this?" When he didn't answer, she turned and saw her cameraman gawking in disbelief at the beast on the other side of the glass.

* * *

Jack could hear Nora in the kitchen, setting the table for an early dinner. He was sitting in the living room, reading the Rocklin Falls Gazette, the town's community newspaper. It was refreshing to see that no one had reported a cryptid sighting or an attack in over two weeks. No Thunderbirds, or Bergman's bears, not even a Bigfoot. He figured the few creatures still alive after escaping the zoo had wised up and were staying clear of hunters, hiding out somewhere in the mountainous forest.

"Can I help you in there?" he called out.

"No, I'm almost done," Nora replied. "It'll be ready in ten minutes."

Jack folded up the paper and tossed it on the coffee table. He turned on the TV with the remote control, as it was almost time for the world news. His favorite anchorman, Lester Williams, was on. The American journalist introduced a lead story and the screen changed, showing two women standing inside a large room with pillars. Jack recognized Jenny Lee, the network's global roving reporter. He had no idea who the Chinese woman was being interviewed.

The sound was turned down low so Jack could hear Nora so he was half-listening to the broadcast. He caught snippets of what they were saying. He glanced back over his chair. "Sure you don't need any help?"

"No, for the second time," Nora answered.

Jack turned back to the TV. "Holy shit!" He immediately put the image on pause. "Nora, get in here!"

Nora stepped into the living room, wiping her hands with a dishtowel. "Keep this up and you'll never get—" She froze when she saw the TV screen. "Oh my God. I went to UC Davis with her. That's Luan Chang."

"Forget her," Jack said. "Look what's behind them." He got up from his chair and moved closer to the flat screen TV over the fireplace mantel.

Nora stepped beside him and grabbed his arm. "Oh my God! That's Lennie in the background."

"It sure is," Jack said.

"Where in the world is this being televised?"

"You're not going to believe it. They took him to China."

10

DARK SECRETS

Even though Amy's father had scored a good deal on the tickets, the only drawback was that he hadn't been able to book their seats together. Caroline was by the window overlooking the wing with Amy sitting next to her in the next seat. An elderly woman occupied the third seat in their row and was wiling away the time knitting a scarf. Gabe was in the row across the aisle.

Amy couldn't help noticing that Gabe seemed out of sorts and chose to sleep even though he had movies to watch and music to listen to on his laptop during the 14 hour-long flight.

She turned and gazed out the window at the white cumulous clouds, knowing that 30,000 feet below was nothing but ocean. Even though she didn't have a fear of flying, the thought of crashing in the middle of the Pacific had her slightly unnerved. She looked down at the in-flight magazine that Caroline was reading. "Anything good?" she asked her friend.

"There's an interesting travelogue and some nice pictures about the ten best beach resorts in Spain. Want to see?" Caroline asked.

"Maybe later."

Caroline stuffed the magazine in the backseat pouch. She reached up and twisted the overhead vent to get some fresh air.

Amy glanced over at Gabe. He was still sound asleep. She turned to Caroline and said, "Is Gabe mad at me?"

"What do you mean?"

"Ever since we arrived at the airport and got on the plane, he hasn't said much to me," Amy said.

"I think he really wanted us to spend some time with his parents during spring break." Caroline patted Amy's knee. "I guess I never told you about what happened to Gabe, have I?"

"Something bad?"

"Worse than bad. Can you keep a secret?"

"Sure," Amy said.

"I mean you have to promise. You can't tell anyone or he'll know I told you."

"I promise."

"You've heard about Cryptid Zoo, right?"

"Everyone has."

"Well, Gabe and his parents were there that weekend."

"Oh my God."

"Gabe saw some terrible things that really messed him up. He was in a psychiatric institution for months afterward. He says he still has nightmares."

"I had no idea."

"He thought for sure they wouldn't get out of there alive. They even got one of his friends."

"That's awful."

"Even now, he hears the word *cryptid* and he freaks. This vacation might do him a world of good. I think I'm going to stretch my legs and use the restroom," Caroline said, unbuckling her seatbelt. She stooped so she wouldn't bump her head on the overhead.

"Sure," Amy said. She tucked back her legs so Caroline could squeeze by and edge past the elderly woman's bony knees. Caroline tapped Gabe on the shoulder but he didn't wake up. She started up the aisle toward the front of the plane.

Amy stared over at Gabe and suddenly felt a pang of panic. It had been so difficult keeping her big surprise from Caroline and Gabe and not blurting it out, which was the main reason for taking this trip.

And now it was about to blow up in her face.

11

FANCY MEETING YOU

Anna Rivers and Mack Hunter sat near the front of the plane two rows down from the lavatories and were working busily on their laptops resting on the dropdown trays. The seat between them was vacant except for the travel case used for carrying their computers and important case files.

Anna turned her computer so Mack could see the screen. "Here's Wilde on the NNCP," Anna said, referring to the National Name Check Program the Federal Bureau of Investigation used to keep track of individuals who might be a threat to national security.

"So when did he arrive in Hangshong?" Mack asked.

"A day ago." Anna took a manila folder from the workbag and opened it on the keyboard of her laptop. She took a loose photograph of a young Asian man and showed it to Mack. "This is Congressman Harvey Tran's son. Joey Tran, birth name Rong Tran. He's an exchange student."

"Not often you see a Chinese-American go to his country of origin to further his education. So how long has he been missing?"

"Over 72 hours," Anna said. "Normally, he face-chats with his mother every day. When they hadn't heard from him, they got worried, and Congressman Tran notified the Bureau."

"Let's hope Interpol has something on his disappearance. Looks like we're going to have a full plate with chasing down Wilde and finding the congressman's son," Mack said. "That is if the boy hasn't surfaced already."

"I don't believe this," a woman said excitedly. "Special Agents Rivers and Hunter?"

Mack looked up. "Caroline. What a surprise. Here, come join us." He grabbed his laptop and closed up the dropdown tray. Anna removed the workbag off the seat so Mack could move over and offer his seat to Caroline.

"It's so good to see you," Anna said. "How is your family?"

"They're fine, thank you," Caroline said, sitting down. "My mother keeps busy and my father is working hard passing bills in the Senate."

"Your sister?"

"She's good."

"So what takes you to Hangshong?" Mack asked.

"I'm on spring break with some friends."

"How exciting," Anna said.

Caroline's face turned solemn. "I need to ask you. Is he..."

"If you mean John Paul Elroy, you needn't worry. He's locked up good and tight in a supermax prison," Anna said, trying to ease Caroline's mind after she and Mack had rescued the teenager from the serial killer clown that had abducted Caroline almost a year ago.

"I have to tell you, I still have trouble sleeping," Caroline confessed.

"If it's any reassurance, just know that he will never breathe air as a free man ever again," Anna said.

"Not with four life sentences," Mack said.

"We're staying with my friend's relatives. Maybe we could see you guys while we're there?"

"We'd love to," Anna said, "but we're working a case."

"Two cases actually," Mack said.

"Here, take my card." Anna gave her business card to Caroline. "Let us know how you're getting on. Even if you just need someone to talk to. I'm always a good listener." She looked over at Mack. "Isn't that right?"

"If you say so."

A lavatory door opened. A teenage boy with a face full of zits stepped out.

"I better grab that," Caroline said. "It was great talking to you guys."

"Take care," Mack said.

"Enjoy your vacation," Anna said.

"We will." Caroline jumped up and made a beeline for the lavatory.

12

HUAN CAT

Jack and Nora had been fortunate enough to snag the last two available seats for the trans-Pacific commercial flight due to no-shows and last-minute cancellations.

Neither of them had ever heard of Hangshong Province before watching the news report on the television.

Nora sat by the window with the sunscreen pulled down, searching various websites for information about their destination.

"So what's this place look like?" Jack asked. He was sitting in the middle seat and had to lean toward Nora as the burly man in the aisle seat was hogging the armrest.

Nora passed her phone.

Jack used his index finger and flipped through images taken of the large city and the surrounding countryside. "Any pictures of this Cryptid Kingdom?"

"Exit that page then scroll down and you'll see it."

After a few taps on the screen, Jack found the appropriate website. At first it looked like a combination of a Six Flags amusement park with a death-defying corkscrew roller coaster and a Raging Waters aquatic park with tubular waterslides with splash pads, a wave machine, and large swimming lagoon.

There were pictures of Chinese temples and pagodas, the grounds landscaped with lily ponds and gardens, surrounded by a fortified barrier constructed of brick and stone that looked remarkably like the Great Wall of China.

As he went down the page, he realized it was more than just a family theme park.

"Did you see these?" Jack asked, gazing at the ink drawings.

"I did," Nora replied.

"Any idea what they are?"

"I recognize some of them. They're Chinese cryptids. I suspect Dr. Chang created them."

"The one you went to school with?"

"Luan, yes."

"What was she like?"

"We shared a dorm room together, if you can believe that?"

"What do you mean?" Jack asked.

"Luan's father is one of the wealthiest businessmen in China. There's nothing he couldn't buy her. Luan was smart, funny. She never acted any different than the rest of us. We grew to be close friends. But after we graduated, she moved back home and I never heard from her again."

Jack continued looking at the animal drawings. Each sketch seemed to get stranger and looked like something out of a child's imagination.

Nora looked down at the screen. "I can't believe Luan actually pulled that one off."

"What is it?"

"It's called a Huan Cat. Click on the short video."

"You mean these things are actually real?"

"They are now," Nora said.

Jack tapped the white triangle in the center of the video frame. At first the large feline looked like a normal lynx from the side view as it walked slowly. Then Jack noticed that it had three tails instead of only one. He was about to comment when the large cat turned its head. It had only one eye and it was in the center of its forehead. The video stopped, as it was only ten seconds long.

A brief description below the video frame stated the creature's hide had the ability to cure a person of jaundice, if worn, and the Huan Cat was prophesized to bring good fortune.

"That is definitely weird," Jack said.

"Think that's weird, wait till you watch the other videos," Nora said. "They'll totally blow you away."

13

OOPSY DAISY

As Carter Wilde's Chief Operating Officer, Lucas Finder was accustomed to his boss's opulent way of living and was not surprised to see the same grandiosity that evening when they pulled up to the front entrance of the luxurious Chang Empire Building.

A bodyguard got out of the front passenger side and opened the rear door so Wilde could exit the limousine. Dr. McCabe climbed out next, followed by Finder. The driver, who was the second bodyguard, turned off the engine and got out as well.

A black SUV pulled up behind the limousine. The four Cryptos piled out. As usual, they were dressed in black, wearing balaclavas and hoodies, and looked like a gang of cat burglars.

Set in the middle of a large square filled with majestic fountains and scatterings of floodlit trees, Chang Empire Building's unique bullet-shaped design prominently stood out from the other modern structures in the Hangshong Province financial district.

One hundred stories tall, the skyscraper was made up of two separate layers, the nose a polished aluminum with the rest of the cylindrical high-rise covered with 5,000 translucent glass panels, and when lit up with multi-colored lights, illuminated the city around it like a kaleidoscopic lighthouse.

The two beefy bodyguards marched over and flanked Wilde as they stepped through the automatic doors into the extravagant lobby with lush furniture arranged in separate sitting areas. Finder and Dr. McCabe were right behind, followed by the Cryptos.

Not only was the Chang Empire Building the corporate headquarters of Henry Chang's conglomerate, the entire top floor was his penthouse home.

As they walked through the separate seating areas reserved for small business gatherings, Finder noticed heavy security staggered about the perimeter. He counted maybe twenty men sharply dressed in business suits, their jackets open slightly for easy access to the side arms strapped on their belts, watching them warily like they were a pack of lions sneaking up on a herd as they passed across the room and headed for the bank of elevators.

A man in a tailored suit stood by the elevator doors. When they were almost ten feet away, he put up his hand like a traffic guard. "I am Kang Wu. Mr. Chang has instructed that only you Mr. Wilde, along with Dr. McCabe and Mr. Finder, are to be allowed up."

"What about—" Wilde started to say but was abruptly cut off.

"Only you three."

Finder could tell that Wilde was fuming. His boss wasn't used to having someone talk to him like that, especially someone he thought as a minion.

Wilde's bodyguards took a step forward to challenge the man.

Chang's security team moved in immediately. No guns had been drawn but everyone had their palms resting on their handgrips. Kang Wu defused the escalation by motioning the men to step back.

"Easy there, boys. This isn't the wild west," Dr. McCabe said, like he was the town marshal breaking up a bar fight in a saloon.

Finder glanced over his shoulder but it was impossible to read the expressions on the Cryptos with half their faces covered. He never trusted them and prayed they didn't do something irrational to provoke Chang's men.

The bodyguards looked to Wilde for direction. "Go grab something to eat," he told them then nodded at the Cryptos. "And take them with you."

Wilde's entourage backed away reluctantly and headed slowly for the main entrance under the scrutiny of Chang's security team.

The doors opened and the four men stepped inside the glass elevator. Kang Wu pushed a button on the panel and the doors slid closed. The car ascended passing floors with mazes of employee cubicles and office machines.

Once they'd cleared the fortieth floor, the view opened up, and they got their first glimpse of the city lights. By the time they reached the seventieth floor, Finder noticed the cityscape below becoming hazy in the misty night sky.

"While you are here," Kang Wu said, "Mr. Chang would like you to be his guests. He has arranged accommodations for you on the floor directly below his penthouse."

A chime sounded when they reached the 100th floor. The elevator came to an abrupt halt and the doors opened onto an impressive suite the size of a gymnasium.

Kang Wu exited and stood by as Wilde, Dr. McCabe, and Finder stepped out. Wu gave them a bow, got back in the elevator, and pushed the button, closing the doors.

Finder felt as though they had walked into a museum. Twenty Chinese tapestries hung on the walls over finely polished tables, each with ancient sculptured artifacts made of jade and bronze. He counted at least ten Ming vases the size of rain barrels staged around the room along with long-fingered palms in large ceramic pots.

The penthouse was exquisitely decorated with enough chairs and couches to sit over fifty people easily, the layout definitely conducive for entertaining small cocktail and dinner parties.

Henry Chang stood with a drink in his hand by the giant forty-foot wide floor-to-ceiling window that overlooked the city. "Ah, Carter, so nice to see you."

"Henry," Wilde said flatly.

Even though they were cordial, Finder could sense the tension between the two men.

"Let me get you all a drink," Chang said. He turned to a man in a white suit standing behind a well stocked bar that would have rivaled a hotel lounge.

"I'll have a bourbon whiskey," Wilde said.

"Is Pappy Van Winkle's to your liking?" Chang asked.

Finder doubted Wilde could turn down a glass from a $3,000 bottle of bourbon.

"Make it a double," Wilde said.

Dr. McCabe walked up to the bar. "A beer." The man behind the counter poured frothy ale into a large stein.

"Mr. Finder?" Chang asked.

Not wanting to appear rude to his guest, Finder rubbed his stomach and said, "Maybe a ginger ale in a bit."

"Rough flight?"

Finder nodded. He walked over to the giant windowpane and gazed down at the tall buildings' rooftops shrouded in the mist.

"I often think I'm staring in the ocean at the city of Atlantis."

Finder turned to the voice and saw a beautiful woman in a Mandarin evening gown, sitting on a couch. She was holding a champagne flute. "Funny, I was thinking the same thing," he replied.

The elegant woman stood. Chang strolled over and put his arm around the small of her back. "Gentlemen, I would like to introduce you to my daughter, Luan."

Wilde raised his tumbler in salutation. Dr. McCabe gave her nod.

"It's very nice to meet you," Finder said, genuinely enamored by her beauty. He gave her a customary bow, which she respectfully returned.

Noticing he wasn't holding a drink, Luan said, "Perhaps you would care for some champagne?"

"Yes, I would, thank you," Finder said and smiled. He walked with her to the bar. A flute of Dom Perignon awaited on the counter. He raised his glass as a gesture of appreciation. "Miss Chang."

"Please, call me Luan, Mr. Finder."

"Very well. Luan. Only if you call me Lucas."

Her smile took his breath away. Finder heard Henry Chang say, "Dr. McCabe, do you have any idea what you are holding?"

Dr. McCabe had picked up a golden vase with carp and flower motifs and put his stein on the table without a coaster. He tossed the antique a few inches in the air as if determining its weight before looking at Chang. "Haven't a clue."

"That was crafted for Emperor Qianlong in the early 1700s. It was originally auctioned for $80 million before I privately acquired the magnificent piece."

The doctor started to return the vase to the table. He bobbled it suddenly in his hands, almost dropping the precious artifact on the marble floor then grabbed it. "Oopsy daisy."

Henry Chang sucked in a deep breath while Luan let out a gasp.

"Joel, quit screwing around!" Wilde hissed.

Dr. McCabe placed the vase on the table and grabbed his beer. The icy stein had left a ring on the polished mahogany.

A man in a waiter's uniform stepped into the room. "Dinner is ready, Mr. Chang."

"Shall we go to the dining room?" Chang said.

Finder watched Chang's eyes narrow as Dr. McCabe and Carter Wilde filed into the next room. He suspected the Chinese billionaire had a low regard for both men, and like all business dealings, their association was purely professional. He hoped he might have a more intimate relationship with Luan but was worried her father might hold the same animosity toward him but then his fears were quickly dispelled when Luan offered her arm for him to escort her into the dining room.

14

ZOMBIE WORM

Henry Chang's hand-carved high back chair was inches taller than the rest in the seating arrangement around the elaborate round dining table and was construed as the head. Luan sat in the chair on her father's left, then Finder, Dr. McCabe, leaving Carter Wilde seated to the right of the Chinese billionaire.

The servers brought out the first entree.

Finders stared down at the bowl in front of him, which was a thick, gelatinous soup. A ceramic spoon was on his place setting along with a pair of plastic chopsticks.

"To begin," Chang said, "we will start with the delicacy of edible bird's nest soup harvested from the limestone caves of Borneo."

Dr. McCabe moved his spoon about in the soup. "Isn't this just bird spit?"

"Joel!" Wilde growled, like he was berating a two-year-old.

Finder knew McCabe was referring to the swiftlets that had the ability of echolocation like bats so they could navigate through caves in total darkness. The birds would construct their nests with strands of their own saliva and cement them together in the shape of small nests, which was the main ingredient for the soup. A single bowl of soup ran about $3,000 and was a $2 billion per year industry.

Finder found the soup to be bland but ate it anyway. Luan seemed to enjoy hers. Wilde and Chang consumed every dollar's worth while McCabe had only a few spoonfuls before pushing his bowl away.

The second entree was generous servings of beef broccoli, Mandarin chicken, steamed cabbage, bok choy, noodles, and steaming bowls of white sticky rice. There was also a large platter of small crabs with orange claws covered with brown fur, and dark green shells, the carapaces maybe four inches wide.

Chang held a crab in one hand, a silver nutcracker in the other. "I hope you enjoy hairy crab." Around the table, the nutcrackers sounded like popping fireworks on Chinese New Year.

This time the culinary experience was much more to Finder's liking. The meat was sweet and tasty. An added bonus was the creamy golden roe inside the shell.

Luan filled a bowl with rice and covered it with vegetables. She looked over and smiled at Finder, then ate a delicate amount of rice with her chopsticks.

Raising his glass of white wine, Chang said, "I would like to take a moment to thank you, Carter, and Dr. McCabe for your contributions. Especially the Yeren, which will be our greatest treasure."

Finder nearly choked and looked up from his meal, knowing McCabe had been unsuccessful in creating the legendary creature and if Chang had one in his possession, it had to have been bioengineered by Professor Nora Howard.

"Our pleasure," Wilde said, taking the credit and hefting his glass.

"What about the Xing-Xings and the raptors?" Dr. McCabe said, not bothering to touch his glass of wine and obviously feeling slighted as he had created those creatures.

"Yes, they will generate much interest," Chang replied. With his glass still raised, he turned to Luan. "And to you, my dear daughter. Cryptid Kingdom would not be possible, if not for you."

"Thank you, father. You are too kind." Luan held up her glass.

Finder, Chang, Wilde, and Luan put their drinks to their lips and paused to look at Dr. McCabe, who still hadn't picked up his glass.

"Joel, we're waiting," Wilde said.

"Oh, what the hell." Dr. McCabe snatched his glass and downed his wine in a single gulp.

The two servers came back into the dining room, carrying tiny plates, which they placed in front of the five diners.

"What is this?" Dr. McCabe said in disgust, studying the thing on his plate.

"I thought you might like to taste another of our delicacies—zombie worm."

"Father, if you don't mind, I would like to send mine back," Luan said.

"If you wish," Chang said.

Finder looked at the shriveled worm on his plate. "What exactly *is* zombie   worm?"

"My father enjoys them but I find them a little too gross," Luan said. "A zombie worm is a worm that has been infected by a parasitic fungi called a cordycep, which has the ability to take over its host and turn it into—"

"A zombie, now I get it," Finder said and looked over at Chang. "If it is all right with you sir, I think I'll pass."

Chang picked the worm off his plate with a forefinger and thumb, put the tiny morsel in his mouth, and swallowed. "I am told cordyceps have many benefits. Sure you won't try some, Mr. Finder?"

Before Finder could answer, Dr. McCabe jumped in and said, "Personally, I like shark fin soup or maybe you have pangolin?"

"I'm afraid those are not on the menu," Chang said. "I don't condone the practice of stripping the fins off of sharks and throwing them back into the ocean to die. Nor do I approve the poaching of pangolins."

"I thought you Chinese ground the scales up for medicine?" Dr. McCabe said.

"My companies no longer deal in the pangolin trade ever since they were put on the Red List of Threatened Species," Chang stated.

"Listen to you," Wilde said with a laugh. "You're starting to sound like one of those radical animal rights activists."

Chang only smiled, letting the comment slide like water rolling off the back of a Peking duck. "Sometimes in order to protect what is dear to us we must make certain sacrifices."

"Father has changed through the years," Luan said.

"My daughter has opened my eyes to many things," Chang admitted, finishing with the course and laying his chopsticks horizontally on his bowl.

Dr. McCabe stood his chopsticks upright in his bowl of rice.

Chang looked at the doctor's bowl and shook his head.

"Did I do something wrong?" McCabe said.

"Not unless you are attending a funeral," Chang replied.

McCabe got the message and laid his chopsticks across his bowl. "So what's for dessert?"

As if on cue, a server came into the room carrying a large tray of five Golden Opulence Sundaes. They ate the Tahitian vanilla bean ice cream and chocolate truffles with gold spoons.

A second server entered with a bottle of Remy Martin and poured the cognac into five crystal snifters.

"Let me," Wilde said. He reached inside his suit jacket, took out a small humidor, and opened it on the table, revealing four cigars inside. Finder recognized the black and yellow band of the Cuban Cohibas, which had been a favorite of Fidel Castro.

"You are so generous, Carter," Chang said when Wilde handed him a cigar.

Dr. McCabe accepted his but Finder declined, as he didn't smoke.

"Let us retire to my smoking room," Chang said, getting up from the table. Wilde and Dr. McCabe rose as well.

Luan turned to Finder. "Would you care to join me on the observation deck?"

Finder looked at Chang. The billionaire smiled, giving his approval.

The three men walked away from the dining table and into an adjoining room.

"Aren't you going to be a little cold out there?" Finder said, gazing at Luan's thin evening gown.

"The cognac will keep us warm."

15

CAT'S OUT OF THE BAG

Caroline spotted a young man waving frantically as they came out of the airport terminal.

"That's my cousin, Tommy," Amy said.

It was especially difficult for Caroline, Gabe, and Amy to weave through the tightly-knit crowd of travelers crammed together at the pickup point as they had to drag their suitcases on wheels.

"Over here, over here," Tommy shouted, jumping up and down to get their attention. He was standing behind a Toyota Corolla amid doubled-parked vehicles waiting to pick up arriving passengers.

"Tommy, I missed you," Amy said, dumping her suitcase by the rear bumper. She gave her cousin a big hug and turned, introducing Caroline and Gabe.

"Nice meeting you. Let me help you." Tommy grabbed Amy's bag and tossed it into the trunk. He then took Caroline's luggage, wedging it between the spare tire. But when he picked up Gabe's suitcase and stuffed it in, he realized he would not be able to close the trunk lid all the way. "Not to worry," he said. He grabbed a short piece of rope, hooked one end to the lid, and wrapped the other end around the car's bumper. "Please hurry and get in the car!"

Gabe opened the rear door so Caroline could slide across the backseat. Amy got in the front seat while Tommy jumped in behind the wheel. Gabe hadn't even closed his door behind him when Tommy—not bothering to look over his shoulder or check his sideview mirror—sped away from the curb into the bustling traffic.

Caroline was shocked to see motorists driving like a bunch of maniacs. Privately owned cars competing with taxis, everyone weaving in and out of lanes in hopes of passing the vehicle in front of them only to brake suddenly in the congested stop-and-go traffic.

"It's like the Daytona 500," Gabe said. He sat back from the window when a small truck got too close and almost sideswiped the Corolla's car door.

They were a short distance from the airport when Tommy entered a roundabout that looped a hillock island and branched off in another direction. He had to slow down as 500 cyclists of every age group funneled onto the thoroughfare. Teenagers, young adults, and elderly people pedaling in unison like a critical mass protesting the usage of fossil fuel in hopes of protecting the planet.

Caroline stared out her window, feeling like a skin diver that had suddenly found herself in the center of a massive swarm of large fish. "Is the commute always like this?" she asked Tommy.

"Oh, no," he replied. "Everyone's going to lunch."

"Are you sure you will have room for all of us?" Amy asked her cousin.

"I have plenty of room."

Amy looked over her shoulder at Caroline. "Tommy lives in a studio apartment."

"If it's too much trouble," Caroline said, "Gabe and I could go stay in a hotel." She looked over at Gabe. He shook his head and gazed bewilderedly out the window.

"So, Amy. I've got awesome news," Tommy said, passing a peloton of cyclists.

Caroline noticed Amy seemed troubled.

"Not now, Tommy," Amy said.

"But I snagged us platinum passes. That means we can see everything."

"What's he talking about?" Caroline asked.

Amy made a face like she had swallowed a bug.

Tommy glanced back at Caroline and Gabe. "She didn't tell you? I got us tickets for the big opening of Cryptid Kingdom."

"Oh my God, Amy," Caroline said. She turned to Gabe. The color had drained from his face.

"Tommy, look out!" Gabe screamed.

16

INTERPOL

Anna and Mack rented a car at the airport and decided to stop at the Interpol office before checking into their hotel. A petite Chinese agent by the name of Li Jing Lee greeted them at the security desk. "Welcome to Hangshong," she said and shook their hands.

"I assume our director filled you in on why we are here?" Anna asked.

"He did," Li Jing replied. She handed Anna and Mack visitor passes on lanyards to wear around their necks. "Please, come this way."

The security guard sitting at the front counter buzzed them through. Li Jing led the way down a long hall and opened the door to her office. "Please, have a seat," she said and motioned to the two chairs facing her desk. She skirted around her desk and sat in a leather swivel chair. "May I get you anything? Tea perhaps?"

"Ah, no thank you," Anna said.

Mack smiled and shook his head.

Li Jing opened a manila folder on her desk. She gazed at the file for a moment then said, "We have confirmed that Carter Wilde is indeed staying here in the city at Chang Empire Building."

"Doesn't that belong to the multi-billionaire Henry Chang?" Anna asked.

"It does," Li Jing replied.

"It's no wonder billionaires flock together," Mack quipped.

Anna leaned forward in her chair. "Wilde is wanted in our country for supplying guns to a radical group responsible for the deaths of several federal agents."

"By the radical group, you mean the Cryptos, am I correct?" Li Jing asked.

"That's right."

"Then you might be interested to know that Dr. Joel McCabe is also with him."

"Well, what do you know," Mack said. "We might be able to get two birds with one stone."

"Dr. McCabe is on our Ten Most Wanted list for multiple murders and escaping from prison," Anna said.

"You do know that Hangshong does not have extradition laws."

Anna and Mack exchanged sideward glances.

"The director never mentioned that. So you're saying you won't allow us to take them back to the States?" Anna said.

"I didn't say that. I'm saying I won't be able to assist you in an arrest."

"In other words, we're on our own," Mack said.

Anna turned to Mack. "I think Li Jing is saying she's willing to turn a blind eye." Anna looked at the Chinese agent to confirm her statement.

Li Jing nodded her head.

"Oh," Mack said, realizing he let that one fly over his head.

Li Jing opened another file on her desk. "I looked into your missing persons report on Rong Tran. He is currently a student at university here. Or was until he went missing. He joins a number of open cases of young people disappearing in our city."

"What, you mean abductions?" Mack said.

"I can't say for sure."

"Any leads?" Anna asked.

"We have narrowed it down to a few possible suspects," Li Jing said. "One being Dr. Haun Zhang."

"What's his story?" Mack asked.

"Ten years ago, while teaching at the university, Dr. Zhang was a person of interest in the strange disappearances of five of his medical students. He fits our profile."

"What happened with the case?" Anna asked.

"Nothing. There was no proof of wrongdoing and Dr. Zhang was never charged."

"And the students?"

"They were never found."

"Where is Dr. Zhang now?"

"Working for Henry Chang."

Anna turned to Mack. "Looks like we have some digging around to do."

"I'll be sure to bring along a very big shovel," Mack replied, shooting his partner a wry grin.

17

YIBIMINS

Mason and Ramsey had just left the eatery and were walking down the passage that would take them to the primate cages when Song pulled up behind them. "Could I get you two to help me?" she asked.

"What do you want us to do?" Mason said.

"We need to inoculate the Yibimins."

"What are those?" Ramsey asked.

"They are some of Dr. Chang's cryptids. She wants to be sure they stay healthy."

Mason looked at Ramsey. "Dr. McCabe never had us vaccinate his creatures."

"That's probably why so many of them got sick."

"Sure, we'll help," Mason said and climbed in the seat next to Song while Ramsey got in the back.

They headed down a tunnel that Mason was not familiar with. A section opened up and he saw a large containment with segregated cages filled with over forty white gibbon-sized monkeys.

Song stopped the electric cart and they got off. Mason and Ramsey walked up to the wire cages.

"Jesus, Mason, what the hell did they do to them?" Ramsey said.

"That's barbaric!" Mason saw that every monkey was missing an arm, some the left, others the right ones.

"It is not what you think," Song said. "They were created that way. We did not amputate their arms. Legend says Yibimins were born as twins, each having only one arm. If left-handed, it was known as a 'throttler' and was able to perform many tasks. If right-handed, it was a 'basher' as the arm was quite muscular. Neither of the twins liked each other and would fight to the death, leaving only one surviving."

"But I don't get it," Mason said. "Why did Dr. Chang create both versions if she knew they would try to kill each other?"

"She didn't," Song answered. "Her Yibimins have learned to mate and have babies."

"Holy shit," Ramsey said. "McCabe could never do that."

They heard two men suddenly arguing in Chinese.

A pen door flew open.

Mason, Ramsey, and Song watched in horror as two screeching Yibimins clashed, a single arm flailing the other. Vicious teeth gnashed and savagely tore into white fur until they were covered with speckled blood splatter like a paintbrush of red paint had flicked them.

Even though the throttler was raining down more blows, it was the powerful punch of the basher that put a quick end to the brawl. The left-handed monkey went down like a KO'd prizefighter, only instead of being rendered unconscious, the creature was stone-cold dead, its face resembling a bloody puddle that a boot had stepped into.

"That was brutal," Ramsey said.

Song walked over and grabbed a towel out of a bucket of water. She opened the pen where the victorious Yibimin stood over its dead rival.

"What are you doing?" Mason said, rushing after Song.

Song turned to Mason and assured him by saying, "Do not worry. It is quite tame. They only fight each other." She picked up the Yibimin and began wiping the blood off of its fur so she could examine its wounds. "While I'm holding it, Mason, would you mind handing me a syringe from that box?"

Mason spotted a metal footlocker with a medical insignia on the lid, positioned next to the fence. He went over, opened it up, and saw packets of already prepared hypodermic needles inside. Taking a syringe out of the hermetically sealed pack, he walked over to Song, and handed her the syringe.

Song jabbed the needle into the Yibimin's thigh.

"Wow, it didn't even flinch," Mason said, duly impressed.

"I used to work in home care for the elderly before I became an animal keeper."

"So you've given shots a million times."

"Well, maybe not that many. Grab some syringes and we can get started."

"What about me? What do you want me to do?" Ramsey asked.

"Would you mind taking those bags to the incinerator?" Song pointed to a flat cart of plastic bags with 'DANGER HAZARDOUS WASTE' stickers. "You can use the scooter. The keycard is in the tray under the steering wheel."

"Sure thing." Ramsey walked over and picked up a number of bags with both hands. He carried them over to the back of the electric cart and deposited them in the rear cargo hold. He went back and got the rest.

Ramsey climbed behind the wheel and goosed the accelerator. The cart zoomed off at a brisk 5 miles-per-hour. A tunnel took him to the door outside the incinerator room.

He turned off the electric cart and grabbed the access keycard. After swiping the reader, Ramsey propped open the door with a yellow cone a maintenance man had left behind, and brought in the bags.

Even though Song had not instructed him to do so, Ramsey figured he was expected to operate the incinerator and burn all of the bags. He noticed two of the laundry carts were already partially filled with burn bags. As he hadn't anything better to do, he decided to spend whatever time it took to dispose of all the bags, even though he had never operated the machine.

He lucked out, as there was an easy-to-understand instruction plate—in both Chinese and English—mounted near the loading door to the combustion chamber. He turned a switch and heard a loud *poof* as the gas jets shot out flames inside the steel housing. He pushed the button that raised the loading door. Already the combustion chamber was billowing heat.

Ramsey began with the bags he had lugged in. He tossed them one by one into the blazing fire. When he was through with those, he began grabbing burn bags out of the laundry carts, and throwing them in.

He snatched up a burn bag and the bottom ripped out. A pair of shoes and some clothing fell to the floor. Ramsey leaned over to pick it all up but paused when he saw a wallet sticking out of the back pocket of a pair of pants. "What the hell?"

Ramsey picked up the billfold and opened it up. He pulled out a MasterCard printed in English, a few yaun bills, some receipts. He was surprised to see a California DMV driver's license with the name Rong Tran.

A noise caught his attention and he glanced up. The yellow cone was scooting out between the edge of the door and the jamb.

Ramsey saw a hand reach around and stop the door from closing.

A Chinese man in a white lab coat stood in the threshold.

"Hey, I'm Todd Ramsey. Who are you?"

"I am Dr. Haun Zhang."

18

CARROT TOP

"You're not going to believe this, but I found some guy's stuff in one of the burn bags," Ramsey said. "Here's his wallet." He showed the billfold to Dr. Zhang who was standing in the doorway of the incinerator room.

"May I see it?" Dr. Zhang asked.

"Sure." Ramsey gave the wallet to the doctor.

Dr. Zhang scrutinized the contents. "Hmmm."

"What do you make of it?" Ramsey said.

"It is curious. Perhaps he worked here and left his belongings behind."

"Strange the guy would forget his wallet, don't you think?"

"We should give it to security." Dr. Zhang put the wallet in his coat pocket.

"All right. I'll go with you."

"Is that your cart outside?"

"I'm borrowing it. It belongs to Song Liu."

"Perhaps you could drive us over. If you don't mind, I must make a stop first."

"Fine by me," Ramsey replied.

Dr. Zhang gave Ramsey an odd look.

"What is it?" Ramsey said. "Something wrong?"

"Your hair. I don't think I have ever seen hair so red."

Ramsey let out a laugh. "Yeah, I know. People kid me all the time, say I look a lot like Carrot Top."

"Who is Carrot Top?"

"He's a comedian. Likes to smash things up on stage. Sort of like Gallagher."

"I don't know who that is."

"Not important. Let me shut down the furnace before we go." Ramsey spent a moment to read the instructions so he could safely turn off the gas flame. He waited for Dr. Zhang to step outside and closed the door behind him.

"So, where to?" Ramsey asked when they had climbed into the electric cart.

"Down that way and turn right."

Ramsey wasn't sure where they were going exactly as he followed the doctor's directions but he had a feeling it was taking them toward the center of the underground facility.

"This is it," Dr. Zhang said.

Ramsey put on the brakes and the cart came to a stop a few feet from a steel door.

Dr. Zhang got out. He slid an access card down the reader, opened the door, and glanced over his shoulder. "Are you coming?"

"Sure, why not." Ramsey hopped off the cart and followed Dr. Zhang into a stark room with a table. He noticed a window and a metal chute on a wall. "What's out there?" he asked and walked over to take a look.

Dr. Zhang came up behind Ramsey and stabbed him in the neck with a hypodermic needle.

"Jesus, what the hell?" Ramsey said, and spun around. He raised his arms to grab the doctor but for some reason his hands wouldn't work. His fingers cramped and curled into claws. He staggered back as his vision became blurry. His entire body suddenly ceased up. No longer able to stand, he fell to the floor. Even though he couldn't physically move or talk, he could still witness what was going on.

Ramsey was afraid he was going to shit himself when the strange man began to undress him. First he took off Ramsey's boots and socks. Then he unbuttoned Ramsey's shirt, and after managing to get it off, he unbuckled Ramsey's belt and loosened his jeans and took them off along with Ramsey's underwear.

Ramsey watched in horror as the doctor bundled up the clothes and boots and put them in a burn bag.

Just like Rong Tran!

He wanted to scream but his vocal cords were paralyzed like the rest of his body.

Ramsey felt completely helpless lying naked on the cold cement floor.

Especially when the doctor dragged him over to the wall, lifted him up, and shoved him headfirst down the metal chute. Even though there was no pain, he knew the impact of hitting the cement must have caused considerable damage to his face.

The dank room looked like a gargantuan compost heap inside a silo. Ramsey figured the deranged doctor would be coming in any moment to bury him in the huge mounds of dirt.

How can this be happening? He kept telling himself—his silent scream echoing inside his head. *Surely this is all a bad dream.*

But then Ramsey realized the nightmare had only begun when tree roots emerged from the dirt and advanced on him like a nest of slithering snakes.

19

CHANG EMPIRE BUILDING

After quick showers in their hotel room, Nora and Jack hailed a taxi and rode over to Chang Empire Building in hopes of talking with Luan Chang.

Once they arrived, Jack paid the driver and they got out of the cab. He craned his head back and gazed up at the monumental 100-story high-rise. "Looks like a damn suppository. Wonder what the architect was thinking when he dreamed this up?"

Nora gazed around at the surrounding buildings, which were more traditional in design. "Does stick out like a sore thumb."

"That's the rich for you. They'll do anything to draw attention," Jack said.

They entered the promenade of garish fountains and staggered rows of cherry blossom trees. People of all ages were sitting around the stone basins, conversing or just enjoying the brilliant sunshine on their faces, radiating down through the canyons of steel and glass.

A slight breeze misted Nora's face as she passed a fountain with a giant stone carp suspended out of the water, the return flow arching from its mouth and back down into the reservoir pool. Thousands upon thousands of tiny, white, coin-shaped cherry blossom petals polka dotted the cement.

Entering the front lobby, Nora saw smartly dressed groups conducting business, seated around the cavernous antechamber. She noticed men in suits that were meant to blend in, but were obviously security guards, standing discretely by the entrance, elevators, and in the corners of the vestibule.

Nora and Jack walked up to the attractive Asian woman seated at the reception counter. "Hello, my name is Professor Nora Howard. And this is Jack Tremens. We would like to see Luan Chang."

"Do you have an appointment?"

"No. Actually I'm a friend of Luan. If you'll just call up and give her my name, I'm sure she'll be more than happy to see us."

"One moment," the receptionist said and picked up the phone.

Nora and Jack waited while the woman conversed in Chinese with someone on the other end of the line. She eventually put the phone down and looked up, her face expressionless like a card player bluffing in a poker game. "If you would kindly have a seat, someone will be right down."

"But didn't you relay my message?" Nora said. "Surely, she remembers me."

"Please have a seat," the woman said curtly.

"Come on, Nora." Jack guided Nora to the nearest available chairs.

"I don't understand," Nora said as she sat down.

"Too bad she wasn't listed, we could have called instead," Jack said. He sat in a chair next to Nora.

The elevator doors opened and a Chinese man in a dapper suit stepped out. Instead of going to the reception desk, he walked directly towards Nora and Jack.

"They must have us under surveillance," Jack whispered.

"Professor Howard," the man said. "My name is Kang Wu. I am the Changs' liaison officer. How may I help you?"

"I was hoping to see Luan Chang. We were friends in college."

"I am afraid she can not see you."

"Why not?"

"For one, she is not here," Wu said.

"Can you tell me where I can find her?" Nora asked.

"I am afraid I am not at liberty to tell you."

"Hey, bub, what's with all the secrecy?" Jack said, unable to contain the hostility in his voice. "We came halfway around the globe to speak to her. Now tell us how to find her."

"I must ask you to leave," Wu said.

"No! We're not leaving until—"

"Jack, stop!" Nora grabbed him by the arm. While they had been arguing with Wu, Nora had noticed the security guards in suits closing in. Jack saw them, too.

"Very well, we're going," Nora said. "Come on, Jack." They got up and were escorted indignantly out of the building.

"I feel like we just got thrown out of the bar," Jack said.

"I don't get it," Nora said. "That was plain rude."

"You don't think they know who you are?"

"What difference would it make?"

"You're a geneticist who creates cryptids. Luan's a geneticist who creates cryptids. For all they know, we came here to steal her patents," Jack said.

"That's absurd."

"Is it? They stole Lennie, didn't they?"

"You're right. What do we do now?" Nora asked.

"I don't know. Go back to the hotel?"

Nora saw a small crowd milling in front of a cylindrically shaped kiosk. "Wonder what's the big attraction?" She walked over with Jack to take a look.

Everyone was chattering in Chinese and pointing at a poster of a massive dragonhead and the words CRYPTID KINGDOM arched over a park entrance.

"I say we forget all the runaround and go there and get Lennie," Jack said.

"Like they're just going to let us waltz in there and take him," Nora said.

"Well, I doubt it will be that easy. You never know, we might even find Luan Chang there. What you've told me of her, I think she might give us a sympathetic ear when she learns how Lennie was abducted from us."

"I'm beginning to have my doubts," Nora said.

20

GLASS FROG

Lucas Finder was duly impressed when Luan showed him around the utility corridor system beneath the soon to be opened theme park. As he had been the project manager of the defunct Cryptid Zoo, he was familiar with many of the functions, such as the AVAC, the automatic vacuum collection process that would transfer trash through pneumatic tubes and deposit the rubbish to a compactor to later be trucked to a landfill.

Luan proved to be extremely knowledgeable, especially when explaining the vast electrical grid that would power the park as they rode by the bank of generators.

Finder was surprised to see shops and eateries that he would expect to see in a shopping mall complex providing services to the 300 employees, many of whom lived in the underground premises and worked in various park operations such as merchandising, maintenance, and food service, as well as cashiers, rider operators, lifeguards, and highly-trained animal keepers.

"Turn left here," Luan instructed the mini tram driver. Once they had gone fifty feet, she told him to stop. She glanced over at Finder seated next to her. "What do you think?" she asked and pointed to a large caged area.

Finder gazed through the tall bars. Five animals stared back at him. "What are they, mules?"

"Look again," Luan said.

He leaned across the side of the tram to get a better look. "Wait a minute. Their bodies are like dogs. But they have the heads of—"

"Donkeys," Luan interjected. "They are Lutoulangs. Donkey-headed wolves."

"That's crazy. Those are actually Chinese cryptids?"

"They are."

A Lutoulang brayed and the other four joined in.

Luan told the driver to continue on.

While they were driving along, Finder could hear animals bleating from a dark side passage. "What's that, sheep or another one of your exhibits?"

"Live food," Luan said.

"Oh, yeah I forgot. I imagine most are carnivorous."

"With great appetites."

The driver slowed the mini tram and stopped in front of a set of glass doors.

"Let me take you through our laboratory," Luan said.

"I'd like that." Finder exited first then held his hand out for Luan to take as she came down the three steps. They went through the pneumatic doors and entered the large laboratory.

Finder recognized most of the test instruments and lab equipment, as they were similar to what Dr. Joel McCabe and Professor Nora Howard had used in their facility when they were conducting their research and experiments at Cryptid Zoo.

Luan stopped at a workbench where two technicians were working. She greeted them in Chinese and they smiled back at her. Finder could tell by the way they beamed they were genuinely fond of Luan. She directed Finder to an enclosed glass terrarium.

He looked inside and saw two snakeheads attached to a single body coiled on the pebbles at the bottom of the tank. "What am I looking at?"

"That is a Feiyi."

"Does it have any significance?"

"Not really, though some think it is a bad omen."

Finder moved across the table and looked inside another vivarium. "I take it this is another variation of the Feiyi?"

"You like it?" Luan said.

"Very creative." The snake inside the glass container had a single head with two adjoining bodies.

"Would you like a coffee?" Luan asked.

"Sounds good."

Finder followed Luan down a corridor and into her office. He glanced around the walls adorned with framed medical certificates and plaques chronicling Luan's academic achievements. "Wow, I had no idea."

"When a father wished you had been a boy, you must learn not to disappoint him."

Finder smiled but felt a little sad for Luan.

"Please, be comfortable," Luan said. She motioned to a cozy leather couch. A glass container was on a coffee table.

Finder went over and sat down while Luan started a Keurig machine. He looked inside the small terrarium. He saw movement but wasn't quite sure what he was seeing, so he kept staring.

Luan brought over two cups of coffee and placed them on the table.

"Is this an optical illusion?" he asked.

"No, your eyes aren't playing tricks." Luan reached in a small box and took out a single plastic glove. She slipped the latex on over her hand, stretched it over her fingers, and snapped it back. She raised the lid on the terrarium, reached inside, and withdrew her hand with the palm up.

Finder leaned forward and saw her holding a tiny frog. But not like any frog he had ever seen before. This amphibian's skin was completely see-through. He could see every organ inside its body—*oh my God look at its tiny heart beating*—even its brain.

"I have been working on a serum that physicians might one day be able to inject in a patient which will render the human skin and surrounding tissues transparent," Luan said. "It would eliminate the need for X-rays. One shot and a doctor could immediately see inside a patient and determine the problem."

"That's truly remarkable."

"Thank you." The glass frog seemed content to remain on Luan's palm. She sipped her coffee and spoke of her other accomplishments in the lab.

Finder listened tentatively, enchanted by this amazing woman.

21

STEAM BATH

A limousine picked Finder up from the park just after nightfall and took him back to Chang Empire Building. He had hoped to spend more time with Luan but she had much to prepare before tomorrow's opening day. Finder had kindly offered his assistance, as he was familiar with the process having done it himself for Cryptid Zoo, but Luan had graciously declined his offer.

He wondered if she was worried he might be a jinx.

Kang Wu was waiting for him when he came into the lobby. Finder didn't particularly care for the man. Wu seemed a little shifty, like someone you might not trust to be alone in your home.

"Mr. Chang has requested you join him," Wu said.

"For what? Dinner?"

"No. It is not good to eat."

"Really. What then?"

"I am to prepare you for the steam bath."

"Okay," Finder said, feeling that was kind of weird. He followed Wu to the elevators. They stepped into the car and rode the lift up to the penthouse floor. Instead of opening on Chang's suite, the doors parted, revealing a large exercise area equipped with treadmills, stationary bikes, a weight room with cardio machines, a squash court, and even a lap pool.

"This way," Wu said. The aide instructed Finder to follow him over to a booth. "You will find towels and a decanter. Drink all the water. Then take a shower. After, you can go in the steam room."

"Gotcha," Finder said. He waited until Wu was gone before entering the changing room. He undressed and hung his clothes on the hooks. He tucked his socks inside his shoes and placed them on the small bench. He entered a glass shower stall and spent a good five minutes washing his body with soap and a coarse sponge.

He grabbed a towel off the rack, dried himself off, and then wrapped the towel around his waist. He drank all of the water from the decanter. He stepped out of the changing room, barefoot, and walked over to the door leading into the steam room.

Finder felt the humidity as soon as he opened the door and stepped on the wooden slats. He opened another door and entered the mist-filled Turkish bath.

Henry Chang sat on a bench, his hair damp and his bare chest and arms glistening from his sweat. For a man in his early sixties, he looked exceptionally fit and probably kept to a rigid schedule using his personal gym on a regular basis.

"Ah, Lucas. Glad you could come," Chang said, as if Finder had just happened along. Henry Chang was a man who demanded punctuality and tolerated nothing less.

"Thank you for inviting me," Finder said. He sat down on the bench, keeping a couple of feet between them.

Chang picked up a metal ladle. He poured water over a mound of hot lava rocks causing a burst of steam to engulf the small room. Finder could feel his pores opening up and the sweat seeping out.

"Think of this like a confessionary," Chang said. "A person absolves his sins with a priest. I indulge and purify my body with a steam bath."

"Good way to rid yourself of what ails you," Finder said.

"Exactly." Chang lifted his feet up on the bench, and leaned back against the wall with his knees slightly spread.

Finder had to avert his eyes from looking at the billionaire's exposed genitalia.

"So tell me. How do you like working for Carter Wilde?" Chang asked, adjusting his towel, sparing Finder the view. "You've been in his employment for some time, is that correct?"

"Five years." Finder knew it was a baited question. The worst thing a person could do was bad-mouth his boss. Because sure as hell, whatever you said, it always came back to bite you in the ass. He could feel Chang's gaze upon him, expecting a proper answer.

"It is not without its challenges," Finder said, trying to stay objective.

Chang let out a blustering laugh. "You mean that damn zoo of his. What a catastrophe that was! I understand that you tried to warn him."

"I did. But he wouldn't listen." Having said that, Finder knew he had let Chang trawl him in. He better tread softly or there would be consequences.

"Well, I know he can be a difficult man at times," Chang said. "I hope our partnering wasn't a mistake."

"Sir?"

"I am offering Carter a piece of the Cryptid Kingdom franchise in return for Dr. McCabe's services. I know that is risky, considering the doctor's history and unpredictability. Which is why I am only giving Carter twenty percent."

"I'm sorry," Finder said. "I wasn't aware Mr. Wilde made such an arrangement." It wasn't the first time his boss had made changes to a deal without consulting his Chief Operating Officer first. And why accept such a petty share; it was embarrassing.

"I have big plans to build parks such as this all over the world," Chang said, reaching for the ladle. He poured more water onto the lava rocks, generating a cloud of steam.

Finder was so flabbergasted he didn't know what to say.

The steam room door opened.

Carter Wilde and Dr. McCabe stepped in, naked except for the towels wrapped around their waists. They sat on the bench directly opposite Chang and Finder in the cloying mist.

"We were just talking about you, Carter," Chang said.

Finder immediately cringed.

"Is that right," Wilde replied.

It was impossible for Finder to read his boss's face in the thick fog.

As the rocks sizzled, the air began to clear.

Finder saw something that sent him for a loop.

He couldn't help but stare at the ugly scar tissue on the right side of Wilde's chest and ribcage. Sitting next to him, McCabe had a similar scar but it was on his left side and a mirror image.

His first assumption was the scars were terrible burns possibly from a fire but then the stark realization suddenly hit him. It explained why Carter Wilde had put up with Dr. McCabe's shenanigans for the past few years. Even when the doctor purposely set out to deliberately ruin Wilde by sabotaging the zoo because of a dispute and causing such a stir at the ribbon-cutting ceremony at Wilde's new high-rise.

The scars were a result of conjoined twins being separated.

Carter Wilde and Dr. Joel McCabe were brothers.

22

XIANGLIU

Mason was frazzled from lack of sleep and rising three hours prior to the park's opening time so he could assist in transporting the creatures to their exhibits. He had waited up till after midnight worrying about Ramsey and wondering where his friend was before resigning himself to the fact that maybe he had met someone and spent the night elsewhere.

Even so, it wasn't like Ramsey not to show up and help with the Xing-Xings, which were his main responsibility, along with the raptors.

Mason voiced his concern with Song earlier that morning. After they had secured the creatures, Mason had ridden around with Song, asking other workers if they knew where the 'redheaded man' might be, as that is how they all knew Ramsey. No one had seen him.

"I swear, Ramsey shows up, I'm going to brain him," Mason said. He spotted a worker running towards them. He was waving his arms and yelling to Song in Chinese.

Song immediately braked the electric cart. She talked to the man in a quick exchange, each treading on the other's words. She ended the conversation by stomping on the accelerator and driving down the tunnel.

"There a problem?" Mason asked.

"Yes! A big one!" Song replied.

They traveled down a passageway and came to an open freight elevator. Every exhibit building on the surface had a service elevator for transporting the animals, along with a spiral staircase. Song and Mason jumped out of the cart and were about to step into the elevator when Mason grabbed Song by the arm. "Jesus, what happened in here?"

The walls were splattered with blood. He saw a framed poster of a dragon with nine heads, which reminded him of the mythical Greek Gorgon, Medusa, that had deadly serpents for hair.

"Seriously? There's a dragon up there?"

"Yes," Song said. "Xiangliu." Her enunciation of the dragon's name reminded Mason of how the Chinese actors would always stress the word 'Godzilla' in the movies.

"Many believe Xiangliu was responsible for the Great Flood of China."

"Damn," Mason said.

"Whenever warriors fought the Xiangliu, the dragon's blood would ruin the land and the farmers' animals would die."

"You really believe that?" Mason asked.

"I do," Song replied adamantly.

"Then why in the world create such a creature?"

"We should use the stairs," Song said, ignoring the question.

Mason took a quick glance inside the elevator. He spotted a crimson pool in the corner of the floor. "Good idea."

They raced up the spiral staircase to the access door identified as DRAGON PAGODA. As soon as Song pushed open the door, Mason heard a chorus of angry roars and a man's horrendous screams.

Mason followed Song into the giant antechamber, half of which was a gigantic cage. The massive cage door was standing open.

He felt like he had just walked onto the set of a Ray Harryhausen special effects movie. The dragon was way bigger than he had anticipated and stood well over ten feet tall at the shoulders. It had scaly emerald skin, a barrel chest, thick legs with sharp talon feet, and a long tapered tail.

Its nine heads undulated in different directions on their six-foot long necks as though suffering from a bad case of cerebral palsy. One of the heads had grabbed an animal keeper in its teeth and was dangling him off the floor. The other heads were taking turns, nipping at the man's body and legs, causing him to scream each time a chunk of flesh was ripped out.

A man was lying on the floor in a large puddle of blood in front of the elevator doors. Mason thought the man was dead but then he saw his hand move.

Six animal keepers advanced, jabbing the dragon with electrode prods. Mason could hear the electrical sparks firing with each contact. But instead of subduing the dragon, the short jolts only made it more furious.

A head swooped down and picked a man off the floor with its sharp teeth. It flung the man in the air. Two heads converged, each grabbing him by a leg, and pulled away.

Mason saw Song turn her face when the man split apart down the middle, his bowels and intestines slopping out onto the floor in a steamy pile.

One of the heads miscalculated and bit into another head's neck. A gush of blood shot about the room, drenching the men. Two more heads attacked the spewing wound, eventually decapitating the flailing head, which toppled onto the floor.

"What are we supposed to do?" Mason shouted to Song, just as a man in a white lab coat and six soldiers in drab green uniforms entered the room from the front entrance.

"Who is he?" Mason asked Song.

"That is Dr. Zhang."

Mason couldn't help notice the disdain in her voice. "Something tells me you don't like him very much."

The multi-headed dragon let out a cacophony of bellowing roars.

Dr. Zhang pointed at the dragon and yelled to the soldiers. They stood side-by-side like a firing squad and raised their rifles, prepared to shoot on the doctor's command.

A woman stormed into the room, also wearing a white lab coat. She yelled at the soldiers in Chinese, who immediately lowered their weapons. She turned to Dr. Zhang and berated him.

"Who's the spitfire?" Mason asked Song.

"That is Dr. Chang. She is the daughter of Henry Chang. He owns the park."

"Looks like she packs some clout," Mason said.

"She also created the dragon."

"That explains it."

Three men raced into the room. Each one carried a high-powered tranquilizer gun. They took aim and fired. Three red-feathered darts struck the dragon dead center in the chest. The fast-acting sedative took effect and the dragon crashed to the floor in a disheveled heap, shaking the foundation.

Dr. Zhang turned and walked out of the building. The soldiers trailed behind him.

Scores of workers poured into the high-ceiling room as Dr. Chang shouted instructions. An emergency response team attended to the wounded and carted off the bodies while a maintenance crew came in to mop up the mess.

The animal keepers worked together and dragged the cumbersome dragon inside the cage so that when the time came and the creature was properly cared for, the door could be properly secured.

Three technicians rushed in with medical equipment to assist Dr. Chang.

Mason watched from across the room while the doctor cauterized the neck where the head had been bitten off and the medical assistants administered a series of vaccinations. He looked over at Song. "What now? They postpone opening the park?"

"We can't do that."

"Why not?"

"Mr. Chang would not allow it. Besides, there would be trouble."

"Trouble from who?" Mason said.

"The people of Hangshong," Song said. "They have been waiting a long time for Cryptid Kingdom to open and would be very upset if it did not."

23

MECCA

Gabe and Caroline got out of the back of Tommy's Toyota but Amy couldn't exit the front passenger side because the handle was smashed into the creased metal of the door after Tommy had struck a car while attempting to veer around a group of cyclists yesterday after picking them up from the airport. She had to wait for Tommy to get out from behind the wheel before she could scoot over the gearshift in the center consol and get out.

Tommy reached back into the car, took out his backpack, and handed Amy hers. He pushed the door closed with his hip and locked it with a key.

Gabe slipped his daypack over his shoulder. Inside were a couple of bottled waters, Caroline and his swimsuits, two towels, a tube of sunscreen, some energy bars and a few incidentals. He looked around and couldn't believe the huge crowds of people—he estimated at least 20,000 that he could see—with more cars arriving and visitors piling out of charter buses and a nearby light rail public transit station, navigating the sea of parked cars in the sprawling lots like a mass exodus of worshipers leaving the city on a pilgrimage to Mecca.

"Are you sure you're okay with this?" Caroline asked.

Gabe stared at the giant dragonhead over the main entrance a distance away.

To be honest, he was feeling a bit anxious. He knew there was an aquatic park and some rides but that wasn't what was bothering him.

It was the animal attractions that had him worried.

While hanging out in Tommy's apartment the previous evening, they had spent some time on the Cryptid Kingdom website so they would know what to expect and plan the outing so they could be sure to see everything while at the theme park.

The short videos of the cryptid creatures had been especially informative. Some of the animals had seemed docile enough but there were those that truly frightened Gabe as they reminded him of the creatures that tried to kill him and his family at the zoo. He couldn't say anything to Amy or Tommy, as they wouldn't understand unless they had experienced the traumatic events themselves. He knew Caroline sensed his trepidation.

"I'll be okay," he lied.

Gabe and his friends soon found themselves caught in the slow-moving flow of park visitors. All around them everyone conversed in Chinese, their short, clipped voices lively with excitement.

"Stay close," Tommy said, holding up their four admission tickets.

Gabe held onto Caroline's hand so that they wouldn't get separated. They moved along like cattle squeezing through a chute to a slaughterhouse.

"Who would have known there would be such a large turnout," Caroline said.

Amy turned and yelled over her shoulder, "That's because this is a big deal. Everyone wants to see these legendary creatures."

It took nearly twenty minutes to reach the admissions booths.

As soon as they had their tickets punched and were inside the park, Tommy suggested they check out the rides first as he anticipated long lines.

Gabe was all for that.

24

TEMPORARILY CLOSED

Gabe was more than happy to let Tommy take the lead, as Amy's cousin was accustomed to dealing with the congested crowds common in Hangshong Province and he had devised a strategy by mapping out different routes they might take throughout the park in hopes of minimizing wait-time in lines; even if it took them off the beaten path.

Tommy led them behind a food concession stand and ducked under a chain strung between two posts.

"Can we do this?" Caroline asked.

"Sure," Amy said, following right behind Tommy. "No one will care."

"Sounds like famous last words," Gabe said, hurrying alongside Caroline.

"I'd hate to get booted out before we even get to see anything."

"We better stay close to Tommy," Gabe replied. He motioned for Caroline to slip under the chain and once she was on the other side, he ducked under himself.

They followed a crude pebbled path presumably reserved for landscapers and other workers that maintained the large garden area. From behind a hedge, Gabe could see park visitors admiring the lush greenery and the magnificent flowerbeds teeming with pink lotus blossoms, yellow and burgundy chrysanthemums, and white orchids amid the dark purple plum trees.

Lily pads floated on an oval-shaped pond filled with orange and white speckled carp lazing on the bottom.

Gabe gazed up and saw pairs of people passing overhead on a slow-moving chairlift like ill-dressed skiers being shuttled to a beginners' slope. A young girl leaned out, looked down, and waved. Gabe waved back.

Moving quickly behind the brush, Tommy stopped suddenly, and raised his hand for Amy, Caroline, and Gabe to wait for his signal. A second later he gave the okay and they emerged out of the shrubs and joined a large crowd that was milling around a fenced in exhibit of long-necked creatures that looked like giant birds.

"What's with the ostriches?" Caroline said.

"Look again, Caroline," Amy said. "Those are dinosaurs."

"What?"

Gabe saw a portion of a sign on the fence that wasn't blocked by people's heads but it was written in Chinese. "You said these things are dinosaurs?"

"Yes. They are called Alxasaurus," Amy said, reading the sign.

"I had no clue dinosaurs had feathers," Gabe said, noticing the green plumage.

They gradually moved along until they reached the other side of the enclosure where they saw a group of smaller raptors covered with blue feathers and red-tipped wings. They had large beaks with tiny teeth and clawed fingers. Each one had a mane of black hair running down the back of its head and neck like the plume on a Spartan helmet.

Amy gazed up at the sign. "These are called Caudipteryx."

"They look like giant roast duck," Tommy said. He turned and led them down a walkway, jostling through the crowd.

Gabe heard a thunderous sound and loud screams. He hadn't realized that they were walking under the steel trusses until he gazed up and saw the heads and shoulders of the passengers inverted on the roller coaster coming into a corkscrew turn. Even though they were a good twenty feet above, Gabe felt like he could reach up and touch them. He continued to watch the car of screaming riders loop into another turn and disappear down the track.

"Pretty scary, eh?" Caroline said.

"Nah," Gabe replied. "Piece of cake."

"Ah, darn," Tommy said.

"What's wrong?" Amy asked.

"I was really looking forward to seeing the dragon."

"Why, what's wrong?" Caroline asked.

"This is Dragon Pagoda," Amy said, and pointed at the sign set up on the front steps. "It says 'Temporarily Closed.'"

"That's a bummer," Gabe said, somewhat relieved.

25

SKY-HIGH

After waiting in line for more than forty-five minutes, Jack was glad their hotel had been able to make a foreign currency exchange so they wouldn't have any hassle buying admission tickets into Cryptid Kingdom with US dollars.

"Did I hear you right?" Nora said, overhearing Jack's surprise when he was told how much the tickets would be from the woman in the booth. "Two thousand yaun to get in? That's around $140 apiece."

"You'd think we were buying Forty-niners season tickets at Levi Stadium," Jack said, handing Nora the tickets while he closed up his billfold and tucked it in a small tote bag slung under his arm that also contained their passports and other identification.

"I've never seen so many people," Nora said, trying to avoid the mob of park visitors veering around her like she was a boulder in the middle of a fast-moving river.

Jack consulted a park map he had been given along with the tickets. "Come on, let's head this way." Grabbing Nora's hand, they merged into the swarm.

But after a few minutes, Nora could sense that Jack was getting frustrated having to deal with so many people. Especially when they reached their major objective, which looked like an ancestral temple with three swooping roofs covered with orange tiles, and orange cement steps leading up to an archway entrance and saw the line out front that stretched for hundreds of people.

"So that's Yeren Temple," Nora said.

"Yeah, and you can bet anything Lennie's inside."

"It'll take forever to get in there."

"Maybe we could figure another way in," Jack said.

"What, sneak in the back?"

Jack glanced at the map then pointed up at the chairlift passing overhead. "Sky-High is just ahead. I bet we could get a good bird's-eye view from up there."

"Might give us some ideas."

"Worth a shot."

Heading in the direction of the nearest chairlift platform, they passed by a long fenced-in enclosure and saw a small herd of majestic white deer, each sporting two-antler racks.

Jack glanced at the sign with a caricature of the animal with a description both in Chinese and English. "So that's what a Fuzhu looks like."

"Like you even know what a Fuzhu is," Nora said. "Look, they even have some Chinese Water Deer." She pointed to a pair of hornless brown deer. Each one had two large incisors jutting down from their upper lips.

"What's with the teeth?" Jack laughed.

"They're also known as vampire deer."

"Okay. So what next?" Jack asked. "Buffy staking Bambi in the heart?"

"Nothing would surprise me here."

26

COBRA FURY

Even though he had ridden the historic wooden 55-mile-an-hour Giant Dipper on the Santa Cruz boardwalk and the hair-raising 76-mile-an-hour steel roller coaster X2 at Six Flags Magic Mountain, neither rides prepared Gabe for the supersonic corkscrew roller coaster Cobra Fury that claimed to accelerate from zero to 90-miles-per-hour in 3.5 seconds.

Gabe stood with Caroline, Tommy, and Amy on the boarding platform and watched the train of thrill seekers propel down the track to the sound of dramatic music blaring over the hidden speakers.

Even though Gabe hadn't heard the roar of jet engines, he could have sworn the train had rocket propulsion the way it took off like a missile.

"Man, did you see that baby go?" Tommy said. He was the first one in a long line to board the next train. Amy stood directly behind him. Gabe and Caroline were in the next parallel line so they could sit directly behind the two cousins for the next ride.

"I'm surprised it didn't fly off the tracks," Amy said.

"The wheels on the track are magnetic," Gabe said. "Has to be for the corkscrews."

"How do you know that?" Caroline asked.

"From *Final Destination 3*," Gabe said. "Not that it did any good. The train still flew off the tracks and they all died." He noticed a worried look come over Caroline's face when he mentioned 'they all died.' "That's not true, they didn't really die, at least, not at first. I mean..."

Caroline put up her hand. "Don't say anymore. I saw the movie."

Gabe wished now he hadn't mentioned the disaster film because different scenarios were beginning to play out in his mind of weird ways they would die. Everyone pushing in line anxious to get on the ride just as the next train pulls into the platform and Tommy falls on the tracks, the steel wheels running over his neck and ankles; Amy getting ejected from her seat as they go into a spiraling corkscrew; Caroline's shoulder bar suddenly opening and she's decapitated when she hits the ground.

He was about to imagine his grotesque death when a loud screech sounded to his left and everyone's heads turned as a train pulled in and came to a sudden stop next to the platform. The shoulder bars raised up in unison and the riders began to disembark, some with horrified looks on their faces, others laughing, a few even in tears. Gabe watched them grab their stuff and scurry toward the exit, speaking excitedly in Chinese.

A bell sounded and the barrier bars swung open, allowing two people to step out of each line and climb down into the train. Gabe counted twelve rows of seats. Tommy and Amy were in the very first row, Gabe and Caroline in the second. As there was no carry-on bags or loose items allowed on the ride, everyone that had them were told to toss their belongings on the other side of the platform and they could retrieve them after the ride was completed.

Even though the seat was contoured and padded, Gabe could feel the hard impact plastic underneath pressing against his shoulder blades and spine.

Tommy glanced over his shoulder with a big grin on his face. "Hey, guys. Nice knowing you." He flinched when Amy punched him in the arm.

"Be nice, Tommy!"

Before Gabe could respond, his shoulder harness swung down and pinned him to his seat. He looked over at Caroline. She was clutching hers with both hands.

"You okay?" he asked.

"I'm not too keen on these kinds of rides."

"You should have said something."

"I'm fine. Really," Caroline said.

"You sure? We could always tell the—"

A loud horn sounded, signaling the ride was about to begin.

"Too late now," Caroline said.

The train suddenly catapulted down the track like a projectile propelled from a slingshot, thrusting Gabe back into his seat. He felt the wind slapping his face, the high-speed acceleration pressing on his chest; the force much like what a fighter pilot trainee would experience spinning around in a high g-force centrifuge. It was difficult to turn his head, but he was able to see Caroline. She looked positively scared out of her mind.

They were going so fast that everything to the left and right of him was a peripheral blur. He could see the crowns of Tommy and Amy's heads and blue sky.

The train went into its first revolution and he spun upside down and around, his stomach shooting up into his throat as the air went out of his lungs and his head became a helium balloon: everyone screaming, Gabe being the loudest.

Get me the hell off this thing! Gabe thought, panic-stricken, knowing there were seven more corkscrew turns up ahead as the train thundered down the track.

27

WUHNAN TOADS

The ride operator signaled for Jack and Nora to step on the white line on the floor. As soon as they were in position, a two-person chairlift came from behind and scooped them off their feet onto the seat. A safety bar swung down and clamped over their thighs as they left the platform and moved along the ropeway fifty feet up in the air.

Jack consulted the park's map in his hand with the view down below. "That's Yeren Temple to the left," he said, pointing at the building as they passed over the natural savannah setting of the deer enclosure. "The next one is Fu Lion Pavilion."

Five minutes into the ride, he pointed out the two-story Birdhouse as they approached the loop that would take them back around.

"Oh my God," Nora said. "Look at that." She was motioning to Splash Down, the aquatic portion of the park on the other side of the grounds with over 2,000 bathers, some wearing life vests, most of them with inner tubes around their waists, floating in the crystal blue chlorinated water in the gargantuan pool section.

"That's insane," Jack said. He watched the wave machines generate a powerful surf so strong it lifted everyone on its crest like a bobbing kelp bed and sent them crashing into one another like bumper cars slamming together in a horrendous pileup.

"It's a wonder no one gets hurt," Nora said.

"Or drowns." Jack flipped the map over in his hands and checked the back page for additional park information. "Says here the wave pool measures 100 by 230 feet and holds 6 million liters of water."

"Which would be roughly," Nora paused a second to make a mental calculation before continuing, "a million and a half gallons."

"Aren't we the brainiac."

Rounding the loop, Jack heard a loud roar and looked over his shoulder as the roller coaster rocketed down the track with everyone on the train screaming at the top of their lungs as though they were plummeting to their deaths into the Grand Canyon.

"Think they're having fun?" Nora said, glancing at the steel trestle track that wrapped around the park.

"Doesn't sound like it," Jack replied.

The chairlift suddenly came to a stop.

"Please don't tell me we've broken down," Nora said.

"Hope not." Jack saw a tall stanchion with a ladder attached about forty feet ahead and half the height as their suspended chair, which gave them an excellent view of the man standing on a round rostrum on the top of the pole.

"What's he doing?" Nora asked.

"I don't know but he's drawn quite the crowd."

Two hundred or more spectators were seated on the bleachers outside a fortified fifteen-foot high wire-mesh fence and were staring up at the man. Next to the man was a long boom with a cable that stretched down to the ground where three men stood around a large wire cage.

The man on the rostrum held a control box and pushed a button. The cage slowly rose off the ground on the cable.

"What do you think is in there?" Jack asked.

"Oh, I don't believe this," Nora said.

"What?"

"Take a look."

Even though they were fifty feet below, the four amphibians were enormous, each as big as an armored tank.

"Tell me those aren't real," Jack said.

"Seeing is believing. Those are Wuhnan Toads."

The albino toads reminded Jack of Jabba the Hutt because they were so rotund and had gigantic mouths large enough to gobble up a dairy cow.

The cage finally reached the end of the cable and hovered beneath the boom. The man on the rostrum operated the control box and the boom swung around so that the cage was hovering over the giant toads.

"What is that?" Jack said. "A beaver? But its tail looks like a—"

"It's a bamboo rat," Nora interjected. "They don't come any bigger than that."

"But what's he going to do with it?"

Nora didn't have to answer because at that moment the man pushed a button and the bottom of the cage opened like a trapdoor, dumping out the large furry animal.

The toads saw the plummeting fat morsel and scrambled like a bunch of infielders converging on the same fly ball, two of them shooting out their tongues and getting tongue-tied.

One toad actually clambered onto the back of another toad, catching the rat in its mouth, which quickly enraged the others. The toads attacked each other like a tag team of Sumo wrestlers while the spectators in the bleachers cheered like a bloodthirsty crowd in an arena, watching gladiators fight brutally to the death.

Jack watched in amazement. "I bet PETA would have a field day if they saw that."

"I don't think rules apply here," Nora said.

The pulley engaged above their heads and the chairlift resumed moving.

Jack glanced down beyond his dangling feet and saw the sprawling branches of a massive tree with a crown spread of 100 feet. "Jesus, even the trees are incredible."

He spotted an electric golf cart coming out of an entrance behind a facade on the border of a garden area and nudged Nora. "Could be our way in," he said.

"Worth considering," Nora agreed.

28

LAUGHING FRUIT

Song drove the utility cart while Mason rode up front, shouting to the people blocking their path to move out of their way, though they had no idea what he was saying as they didn't understand English.

"You must learn to be patient," Song said.

Mason quickly caught on and stopped ranting like a loon. "Wish I had a copy of *Chinese for Dummies*. Sure would make my life a lot easier," Mason said, though he was doubtful a tutorial would help him better understand the fast-speaking language.

Song drove off the main walkway to avoid the park visitors and turned down a narrow lane that took them to the service entrance of Yeren Temple cordoned off by six-foot tall chain-link fencing with slats. Mason climbed off the cart and followed Song to the back door where she swiped her keycard down the reader. The deadbolt latch disengaged and the heavy metal door opened onto a narrow corridor that ran behind the main exhibits.

They went down the hall to a short flight of stairs that took them up to a landing where they could look through a window undetected and see inside the observation area.

Mason could hear the park visitors packed shoulder-to-shoulder, clamoring on the other side of the glass, everyone moving in a painfully slow procession to get a decent look at the majestic Yeren in its museum-like habitat and the rambunctious Xing-Xings running wild inside their glass-faced enclosure.

The Yibimins were in separate exhibits so that the lefties and the righties could be segregated and wouldn't try killing each other, which would have been a gory sight to behold and might have made a popular attraction, watching two one-armed apes beating each other to death.

Mason gazed down and spotted Lennie hunkered in the back of his exhibit. It was difficult to tell if the giant Chinese ape-man was afraid of all the people pressing up against the glass—especially those pounding rudely to get his attention—or if he was in a deep depression from being confined and put on display. If Mason had his way, he would have liked nothing better than to go down and free the big brute but that wasn't his call.

"We can come back later?" Song said. She gave Mason an empathetic look, as she shared the same sentiment with many of the creatures she cared for.

"Sure, let's go." Mason went with Song back down the stairs and outside to the utility cart. They drove off and soon found themselves caught in a slow-moving tide of park visitors. A large congregation was gathered around the colossal Jinmenju tree.

Mason could hear ruckus laughter. "What's everyone laughing at?"

"It's not the people. It is from the tree."

"You're telling me the tree's making that noise?"

"Actually, it is the fruit hanging from the branches."

"Pull up closer and stop," Mason said. When they were close enough, Mason stood on the passenger seat so he could see over everyone's heads and get a good view of the tree. He gazed at the hanging fruit on the branches expecting to see something that resembled mangos or coconuts. Instead he saw what looked like human heads and they were all laughing. "You've got to be kidding me. That's creepy!"

"They say," Song said, "if the fruit laughs too hard, it will fall to the ground."

"You expect me to believe—" Mason paused when he heard a familiar horselaugh. Then came the sound of something crashing down through the branches and a thud on the ground.

Mason watched in horror when a large piece of red fruit rolled down the slope and came to a stop.

It looked just like Ramsey's head and it was still laughing.

29

FU LION PAVILION

Gabe had a slight headache and felt queasy after riding the gut wrenching roller coaster, Cobra Fury. He knew Caroline wasn't feeling any better but at least the coloring was returning to her face. Tommy and Amy acted as though the terrifying ride had been no big deal and even tried convincing Gabe and Caroline to go again.

As there was still so much to see and they still wanted to spend some time at Splash Down, Gabe convinced the cousins that once they left the water park, they could tackle Cobra Fury again, even though he had no intention of doing so.

Their next exhibit was Fu Lion Pavilion. As they moved up in the long line, Gabe noticed the two giant statues out front of the building. "What's the significance of the lions?" he asked.

"Those are Fu Lions," Tommy pointed out. "In Eastern culture they represent Buddha. Somewhat like your cross represents Jesus Christ."

"What does Fu mean?" Caroline asked.

"Fu means blessing," Tommy said. "Fu Lions represent prosperity."

At first glance, the two statues looked like identical bookends but as the line moved up the steps and Gabe got closer, he noticed there were a few differences in the way the Fu Lions had been sculptured even though they both looked fierce and wore armor bands on their forelegs and had manes of steel balls. "They're not exactly the same; why's that?"

"That is because the Fu Lion on the right is the male and the other one is the female," Tommy said. "What we refer to as Yin and Yang. You'll notice that the male's right front paw is resting on a globe, which represents life, as it is the man's job to protect the world. The female's left paw is resting on her cub and it is her job to protect her family."

"They are sometimes called the Chinese Guardian Lions," Amy piped in, "and can be found outside important buildings in all of China, even in front of restaurants."

"Wow," Caroline said. "You guys should be tour guides."

"Everyone in Hangshong takes pride in our culture," Tommy said.

Gabe had to admit he was surprised by Tommy's enthusiasm and his knowledge of his historical past, as it was often that new generations did not embrace their heritage and let the old customs slip away into obscurity. "Don't say any more," Gabe said. "Save some for the tour."

They filed inside the building along with the other park visitors. Gabe saw displays with paintings and blown-up black and white photographs of the Hangshong people from ancient times. He stayed close behind Caroline and edged by the rows of manikins dressed like kung fu fighting monks and warriors wearing headgear and suits of armor.

Most of the plaques below the exhibits were in Chinese with only a few with a brief description in English at the bottom, which Gabe found disheartening as he was interested in learning as much about the tour as possible.

A roar boomed inside the massive room, echoed by another roar.

"Oh my God!" Caroline gasped.

Gabe heard over a hundred people react the same way, muttering in Chinese.

Contained in a behemoth cage were two enormous Fu Lions—the spitting image of the statues on the front steps. Their armor clanked as they stomped about, baring their stone-like teeth with each sneering growl.

Gabe gawked at Tommy and Amy. "I thought you were kidding. You mean these things are real?"

The cousins were just as surprised.

30

YEREN TEMPLE

After being stuck in the slow-moving line for almost forty-five minutes, Nora and Jack were finally inside Yeren Temple. The cavernous hall was filled with scores of chattering visitors following the roped-off walkway in front of the animal enclosures.

"I don't believe it," Jack said when they came to the first habitat and he saw the six creatures behind the large plate glass window. "I might be wrong but I think those are the same apes I saw in McCabe's laboratory bunker."

"Really? You think these Xing-Xings are the same ones?" Nora asked.

"Yeah, I'm pretty sure."

"You do know these are only infants," Nora said as they watched the baboon-sized primates loping about their enclosure, pounding on their chests, and redecorating their habitat by ripping out the artificial foliage. "If their DNA code is correct, they should grow to six feet tall and weigh two hundred pounds. They'll be much lankier and their fur should turn a dull black."

"And be just as crazy."

They moved at a snail pace to the next two exhibits.

"Looks like more of McCabe's freaks," Jack said, looking at the one-armed apes.

"No, believe it or not, that's how they are supposed to look. They're Yibimins. I doubt that McCabe had anything to do with their creation. These are probably the work of Luan."

There was a glass partition between the two troops of apes: the lefties on one side, the righties on the other side. Every so often, a Yibimin would glare at another primate in the next enclosure and they would throw their bodies up against the thick tempered glass and screech with ferocity in an attempt to attack one another.

"Oh my God, Jack," Nora said when they moved along to the next habitat. "There he is." She was almost brought to tears when she saw Lennie sitting in the corner, his shoulders slumped and his head hanging down. Many of the people around her were trying to get the giant Yeren's attention by smacking their palms on the glass. Nora was tempted to yell for them to stop but instead, she stood there docile, hoping that Lennie would happen to gaze up and see her.

"He looks like a kid on his first day at the orphanage," Jack said. "It's enough to make—" and then his voice choked up.

When Nora could no longer hold back the tears, she felt Jack pull her close. "Don't worry," he said. "We'll get him out of there."

31

THE BIRDHOUSE

From afar, the structure looked like a typical bird feeder with holes drilled in the walls to allow avian access but as they entered the lower level deck, Gabe realized the circular portals were actually made of lightly tinted glass. As the interior was brightly illuminated, he could see inside and did not have to cup his hands around his face to shield the sunlight. "What in the world are those?" he asked, watching half a dozen owls hopping around the straw covered floor as each bird had only one foot.

"Those are Qizhongs," Tommy said, either having done his research before coming to the park or having read the sign in Chinese posted by the round window.

"Aren't they supposed to be bad luck?" Amy said. "Something to do with plagues."

"I don't know about that."

"What's with their tails?" Caroline asked. "They're coiled like a pig's."

"I have to say," Gabe said, "whoever dreamed these things up had one twisted imagination."

The next exhibit proved to be even weirder.

"This is totally insane," Caroline said and laughed when she looked through the next window.

Gabe peered in and saw ten or more red birds and an equal amount of black birds, each one jumping about on a single foot like the owls in the other exhibit. Each bird had only one eye and looked like it had been cleaved down the center from its beak down to its tail feathers, rendering only half a fowl. "They look like a cruel joke," he said.

"They're ManMan Ducks," Tommy said. "Watch what they do." Just as he said that, a red bird and a black bird joined together like a matching set, flapped their wings in unison, and flew about the small aviary like a single two-colored bird.

"That is wild!" Gabe said.

Gabe and Caroline followed the cousins upstairs with the other visitors to the second level of The Birdhouse.

The first exhibit took up more than half of the top floor and was home to a dozen or more winged creatures. They were as big as cormorants with long bronze beaks and seahorse-like heads. Their segmented bodies had random black and red plates extending down from their long necks to the tip of their serpentine tails.

The strangest thing about them was their wings, which looked like the skin had rotted away leaving large gaps between the blue-colored bones but then there were plumes of green feathers on the outer edge of each wing.

"What the heck are those?" Gabe said, almost wanting to laugh.

"Those are called Zhenniao." Tommy said.

"It's a wonder they can even fly," Caroline said, watching two of the aerodynamically handicapped birds take flight and soar about the room without any problem.

"See those green feathers?" Tommy said. "Legend says that Zhenniaos feed on venomous snakes, which transfers to the feathers and makes them poisonous. If you put a feather in someone's drink, they will die."

"That sounds a little morbid," Caroline said.

Gabe heard excited voices from the group of visitors peering into the windows of the next exhibit, which made him anxious to see what was next.

Even though the lights were not on in the next room, Gabe saw bright flashes zigzagging in the darkness. At first he thought they were streaks of artificially created lightning but then Tommy said they were Sky Serpents.

"They don't have wings," Caroline noted. "It's like the snakes are suspended in thin air. How is that possible?"

"Heck if I know," Gabe said, wondering the same thing.

"Well, what do you say, we go find a place and change into our trunks and check out Splash Down?" Tommy said. "Unless you want to go on Cobra Fury?"

"Let's do the water park," Gabe said, figuring the tamer the better.

32

SURPRISE APPEARANCE

"Do you want to take the lead on this or should I?" Mack said to Anna as they entered the main lobby of Chang Empire Building.

"Knock yourself out," Anna replied.

They walked up to the reception counter, and as a courtesy, Mack presented his business card to the young woman instead of displaying his badge. He gave her a moment to digest the information on the card before saying, "We would like to speak with Henry Chang."

"Do you have an appointment?"

"No, we don't."

"I am sorry. Mr. Chang is a very busy man and can not see you," the young woman said.

"How about you schedule us in," Mack said.

"I will have to check with Mr. Wu."

"You don't understand," Anna said, a little prickly from the woman's attitude. "We're following up on an active investigation on a Dr. Haun Zhang."

The receptionist picked up her phone. "One moment. Let me call Mr. Wu."

Mack and Anna stepped away so the receptionist couldn't overhear them speaking. "Do you get the feeling we're getting the brush-off?" Mack said.

"Big time. And who's this Mr. Wu?"

"Probably some flunky liaison."

Anna looked over Mack's shoulder. "That must be him now," she said, spotting a short man in a business suit exiting the elevator and walking towards them.

This time Mack and Anna were more direct and showed their credentials, identifying themselves as federal agents.

Anna began with, "We believe Dr. Haun Zhang is employed by Mr. Chang. Is that correct?"

"Why do you ask?" Mr. Wu said.

"It's in regards to a criminal investigation," Anna responded.

"Must I remind you that you do not have any authority here."

"Yeah well, that may be true..."

"That is all. Good day." Mr. Wu turned and headed back toward the elevator.

Mack started after him but Anna grabbed his arm when she noticed the doors to another elevator open and Henry Chang, Carter Wilde, and Dr. Joel McCabe stepped out.

"Am I seeing things or did we just hit the jackpot?' Anna said. She was about to suggest that they go up and approach Chang, but then half a dozen security guards in suits gathered protectively around the Chinese businessman, Wilde, and McCabe to escort them out of the building.

Anna and Mack watched the three men walk out of the lobby to a white limousine waiting at the curb along with two black SUVs.

"More like we won Publishers Clearinghouse," Mack replied.

It took a few minutes before the three-vehicle motorcade pulled away, giving Anna and Mack enough time to get to their rental car parked just around the corner.

"Quite the entourage," Anna said as they hung back a few car lengths in the congested traffic behind the black SUV tailing the stretch limousine following the lead SUV cutting through the sea of taxis, compacts, and annoying cyclists like an icebreaking ship. They eventually left the city limits and traveled into the countryside.

Twenty minutes later, Mack was forced to pull off the side of the road when the motorcade ahead was allowed passage through a security gate behind a sprawling visitor parking area filled with over 10,000 automobiles. He stared at the fortress wall a person would expect to see surrounding a medieval castle instead of an amusement park. "So that's Cryptid Kingdom."

Anna watched the limousine and one of the SUVs disappear into an underground entrance while the second SUV doubled back in the agents' direction. "Get down," Anna said and slouched in her seat, catching a quick glance of the driver and the three passengers wearing hoods and balaclavas in what looked like a black Cadillac Escalade passing by.

"Well, what's our move?" Mack said, sitting up straight behind the wheel.

"Right now we can't touch Wilde or McCabe, and our only play is finding Dr. Zhang."

"What about them?" Mack said, staring at the SUV in the rearview mirror, driving down the road.

"They're open game."

"Did you get a good look at them?"

"Oh, yeah. They were definitely Cryptos."

"Wonder what they're up to?"

"Can't be good, whatever it is," Anna said. "You know, any criminal activity would blow back to Wilde by association."

"Which might interest our Interpol girlfriend."

"Maybe get us some special consideration."

"It's worth a shot." Mack started up the rental car, hung a U-turn, and took off after the Cryptos' vehicle.

33

SPLASH DOWN

Wearing their bathing suits, Gabe and Caroline were set to step into the small two-person raft while Tommy and Amy waited next in line. Gabe had elected to wear the elastic wristband with the key to the locker containing their clothes, shoes, and day bags. He gazed out over the platform railing and caught a glimpse of the lagoon where the four tube slides spilled out 80 feet below.

A park operator motioned for Caroline to get in first at the rear of the raft facing forward, then instructed Gabe to sit in the front of the raft facing Caroline. Grabbing hold of the rubber handles, Gabe looked up at the operator and nodded they were ready.

As water gushed out of the ducts and down the chute, the operator pushed the raft over the edge and it shot down the slide into a tubular tunnel with orange walls. Caroline let out a scream as the raft picked up speed, gliding up the side of the curved walls, and then slaloming to the opposite side into a turn.

Gabe remembered his father sharing his experience when he had undergone a colonoscopy procedure and how he was able to watch a TV monitor while a tiny camera navigated his intestinal tract. Gabe imagined it was pretty much like this ride.

They continued to rocket down; Caroline screaming her head off, Gabe laughing all the way until they finally splashed down into the lagoon. Upon impact, the raft spun around and they found themselves drifting into a larger tunnel, only it was clear and appeared to be the concave bottom of an aquarium.

"Wow, this is amazing," Gabe said, staring up at the crystal-clear aquamarine water and seeing schools of fish swimming around him. They were medium size in the range of twenty pounds, and looked like mackerel or bonitoes. He thought it was strange having fish in an aquarium that were better suited on a dinner plate.

"Hey, was that a blast or what?" Tommy yelled from his raft as he and Amy drifted into the tunnel.

"I could hear Caroline screaming all the way down," Amy laughed, shaking the water from her hair.

"I was having fun," Caroline said. "Besides, I only screamed a little."

"Hate to hear what you would sound like if you were scared," Gabe said.

He found out quickly when Caroline's eyes grew big and she let out an ear-piercing scream when a shadow passed over them.

Gabe looked up and saw a gray, seal-like creature with a long neck swoop into a school and scoop up three fish in its mouth with one savage gulp. It was big, at least twenty feet long with gator-like arms and long claws, no hind legs, and a flat paintbrush tailfin, and when its body rubbed against the surface of the glass, Gabe could hear an unsettling sound as though the glass was about to crack.

"What was that?" Caroline yelled.

"I believe that was a Guai Wu," Tommy said. "I saw it on the website. It means 'strange beast.'"

"There're more," Amy said, pointing to five such creatures attacking the other schools of fish.

"Must be feeding time," Tommy said.

Gabe watched the feeding frenzy for a moment longer and then the predators in the aquarium disappeared from sight when the current brought the rafts around a bend to the disembarking station.

A ride operator held the side of the raft so Caroline and Gabe could get out.

"What now?" Gabe asked as soon as Tommy and Amy were out of their raft.

"We should hit the wave machine," Tommy said.

Gabe looked at Caroline. "What do you say? Up for some body surfing?"

"As long as we don't have to swim with those things."

34

KNOCKING ON DOORS

Mason was still upset after seeing what he believed to be Ramsey's head under that damn tree. It seemed so life-like. But how could that be? Surely it wasn't real. The resemblance had been uncanny.

The only rational explanation Mason could think of was that Ramsey was approached by someone that managed the exhibits and had gone somewhere, possibly an offsite studio, to model for the fake fruit and then gotten sidetracked which was why he wasn't around.

There was no doubt that laugh had definitely been Ramsey's.

Again, Ramsey was probably involved in the hoax, recording his horselaugh so that it could be played on a small audio device hidden inside the fruit.

Which meant that all the hanging fruit had been sculptured using volunteers, and their laughter captured on tape. Mason had shared his thoughts with Song, but she admitted she knew nothing about the Jinmenju tree, only that it gave her the heebie jeebies, a term he found comical coming from her.

Still, he wasn't totally convinced.

"Are you all right?" Song asked, parking the utility cart near the bamboo rat cages.

"This is bugging me to no end," Mason confessed. "We need to find Ramsey. Any suggestions where he might be?"

"No," Song said, shaking her head.

"He hasn't been back to the room and we've driven everywhere. Where else could we check?"

"Perhaps Dr. Zhang has seen him. It is his tree."

"It's worth a try. Where would he be?"

"I'll take you to his office," Song said. "It's not far, we can walk."

Mason got off the electric cart and joined Song. He could hear the giant rats crammed together, rustling in the huge cages. The ammonia smell of their urine and the cloying stench of excrement were so foul Mason and Song had to cover their noses as they passed by.

"After we see Dr. Zhang," Song said, "we should move the rats to their staging areas and clean their cages."

"Never thought I would be cleaning up after a bunch of stinking rats," Mason said.

"It is what we do," Song said with a tone of pride.

Mason knew she was the type of person that found honor in everything she did, no matter how menial it might be. He respected her for that and decided that he wouldn't complain anymore as he believed it showed a sign of weakness in her eyes.

They came to a set of sliding glass doors that automatically opened up into a foyer with two doors.

"The door on the left is where Dr. Zhang lives," Song said. "The other door is his laboratory."

"Let's see if he's home." Mason knocked on the door to Dr. Zhang's living quarters. When there was no response, he knocked again. Still nothing.

"Maybe he's working in his lab," Song said.

Mason went over and rapped on the other door.

Again, the doctor did not answer.

"Or maybe he's in but he can't hear us," Mason said. He tried the lever handle but the door was locked. "Well, I guess that settles that."

"I know where he might be," Song said.

"Where?"

"He sometimes goes to the room under the Jinmenju tree."

"What's in there?"

"I am not sure. I have never been inside."

"Won't hurt to take a look."

"We should hurry."

"I know, the bamboo rats," Mason said, knowing Song was anxious to get back and start cleaning their cages. "We'll make this quick."

It took them only a few minutes to reach the circular concrete structure situated in the center of the underground facility.

"If you don't mind, I am going to attend to the cages," Song said. "You will join me when you are through?"

"Sure, that'll be fine. I'll catch up in a minute." Mason watched Song head down the passageway. He turned and pounded on the metal door set in the cement wall.

When no one answered, he got impatient and hammered on the steel with the heel of his fist like he was thumping a drum. To his surprise, the deadbolt disengaged and the door swung open a few inches.

"What do you want?" a voice said from behind the door.

"Dr. Zhang?" Mason asked.

"Yes."

"I'm looking for a friend of mine. Todd Ramsey. You might have seen him."

"I don't think so," Dr. Zhang said, still hiding behind the door.

"Are you sure? He's an American. Average height, red hair."

The door opened an inch wider.

"You said, red hair?"

"That's right," Mason said.

"Are you alone?"

"Yeah."

"Come in."

Mason stepped into the dark room and the door closed behind him.

35

WATCHTOWER

Four watchtowers overlooked the sprawling amusement park. Situated atop the impressive wall, a tower stood on the north end, with two towers in the midsection facing each other from the east and west sides, and a tower at the south end.

Three structures were open to the park visitors, providing everyone a bird's eye view of Cryptid Kingdom. The towers were exact replicas of the ones on the real Great Wall of China, each with a spiral stone staircase leading up to an observation deck surrounded by a parapet walk with fortifying turrets where ancient archers might have stood defending the stronghold.

The tower on the eastern portion—which was ten feet taller than the others—was reserved for Henry Chang and his guests only, and was equipped with an elevator, a lavish glassed-in box seat with plush chairs and a well-stocked wet bar, rivaling the emanates of even the richest sports team owner.

Lucas Finder stood next to Luan Chang at the observation window and gazed out at the colossal water park with its four steep slides, a large lagoon, and the wave machine pool filled with bathers floating in inner tubes. Beyond, he could see the bustling crowds of people enjoying the various attractions throughout the park.

He was particularly drawn to the trestle track of the roller coaster a hundred feet away that ran between the tower and Splash Down. He could hear the riders' faint screams through the glass as the train raced down the track into a complete 360-degree loop and catapulted out of the corkscrew turn.

"I see you are taken with Cobra Fury, Mr. Finder," Henry Chang said, joining his daughter and Finder at the window to admire his newest proprietorship.

"Nice piece of engineering," Finder said. Being Chief Operating Officer of Wilde Enterprises, he was often tasked with heading up various building projects for the company, and unfortunately was the project manager responsible for erecting the dome over the now defunct Cryptid Zoo, an endeavor he would rather forget.

"You are looking at over 2,000 tons and nearly a kilometer of the best quality alloy and factory-formed tubular steel money can buy," Mr. Chang said, "forged right here in Hangshong Province at our own steel mill."

"Again, that's pretty impressive," Finder said.

Seated by the wet bar, Carter Wilde lit up a Cuban cigar. "Lucas, how much steel did we purchase to build Wilde Skyway?"

Finder knew Wilde was trying to get Chang's goat and belittle the Chinese billionaire's accomplishment. "I don't recall."

"Sure you do, Lucas," Wilde said, blowing out a thick plume of smoke.

Mr. Chang turned and looked at Finder.

"Well," Finder said. "If I remember right, it was about 120,000 tons."

"Now, *that's* what I call impressive!" Wilde said. He turned to Dr. McCabe, who was behind the bar adding some ice cubes to a tumbler as he grabbed a bottle of bourbon. "What do you say to that, Joel? That's twice the steel it took to build the Empire State Building."

"Yeah?" Dr. McCabe said, "And what did that fiasco set you back?"

Wilde looked to Finder.

"Twelve billion," Finder replied.

"Twelve billion?" Dr. McCabe said. "You know how many cryptids I could have made with that amount of money?"

Luan turned to her father. "If you will excuse us, I promised Mr. Finder that I would give him another tour of our laboratory."

Chang asked Finder, "Sure you would not like to stay and have a drink with us?"

"If it's all right with you sir, I've been looking forward to seeing more of Luan's work," Finder said.

"Very well."

Luan gave her father a kiss on the cheek and then walked with Finder across the room to the elevator door. Once inside the car and the door had closed, Luan feigned to collapse against the wall. "Why do men always do that?"

"Do what?"

"Think they have to always rattle their swords. There's a Hangshong expression, 'The bigger the elephant's trunk, the easier it is for him to step on it and fall.'"

Finder let out a laugh. "Really, that's an expression? I don't think I've ever heard it said quite that way."

They rode down to the ground floor. The elevator door opened to a passage inside the wall that would lead them to the stairwell to the underground facility.

On their way, Finder noticed a fissure on the brick wall. He stopped to examine the jagged, four-foot long vertical crack made up of crumbled mortar and split bricks all the way down the wall to the concrete floor. There were openings large enough that he could fit two fingers inside. When he took his fingers out, they were damp. "This isn't good."

"What's wrong?" Luan asked.

"Looks like a foundation crack."

Finder heard the sound of dripping water from behind the wall a spelunker would expect when exploring a wet cave. "Do you hear that?" he asked Luan.

"Yes. Perhaps there is a leak of some sort. The water park is just above us."

"Where is the supply?" Finder asked.

"It comes from an underground aqueduct."

"And where is that?"

"Below our feet."

"Damn. How much water is needed to operate Splash Down?" Finder asked.

"I am not sure."

"Two million gallons?"

"Perhaps."

"At seven pounds a gallon, that's 14 million pounds partially resting on an underground facility sandwiched over a depleting aquifer. You've heard of fracking?"

"That's when wastewater is forcibly pumped into the ground to displace petroleum."

"That's right. It's a booming industry especially for natural gas. Only problem, it also undermines the bedrock and causes areas that were once stable to become earthquake-prone."

"Do you think this could happen here?"

"There's a possibility," Finder said. "We should tell your father. Have him bring in some seismic engineers to ensure the park is safe."

"Once I am alone with my father, I will speak to him of your concern. I am glad you noticed it rather than that pompous Carter Wilde," Luan said scornfully then put her hand to her mouth. "I am so sorry to speak ill about your employer."

"It's quite all right," Finder assured her. "Believe me, he's been called a lot worse."

36

SURF'S UP

In order for Gabe, Caroline, Tommy, and Amy to remain together and not drift apart, they had to hold on to the handles on each other's inner tubes while floating in the undulating wave machine pool along with 2,000 other swimmers. Gabe could hardly call it swimming when all you did was bob in the water waiting for the giant pistons at the end of the pool to generate the next wave.

He had hoped to get in some body surfing but it was impossible wearing the inner tube, as everyone was required to use an inflatable flotation device to prevent being shoved below the surface under a ton of people.

Anticipating and timing the next wave, everyone joined in and cheered like adoring fans greeting a famous celebrity on the red carpet.

"Here comes another one," Tommy yelled.

Gabe saw the white water surge build up into a forming wave, then lift the front row of inner tubes up on its crest, sending bathers crashing into the main group like an invading armada.

Caroline's inner tube raised enough that her elbow caught Gabe in the face, striking him in the eye. The wave sent water splashing over everyone as they collided into one another. Gabe saw a small Asian woman flip upside down with her feet sticking up in the air then slip under the water.

This is insane, he thought to himself. *People can actually get killed here!*

Gabe breathed a sigh of relief when a man grabbed her by the arm and hauled her to the surface.

The rolling wave leveled out, sending a few bathers onto the sandy shore of the man-made beach.

Gabe could feel his feet touch the bottom.

"Are you all right?" Caroline said. "Did I do that?"

"It was an accident," Gabe said, cupping his right eye.

"Does it hurt?"

"A little."

"I'm sorry," Caroline apologized.

"No big deal. Want to get out?"

"Sure." Caroline looked at Tommy and Amy. "You guys coming?"

"Give us fifteen more minutes," Tommy said. He looked at Amy to confirm and she nodded that she wanted to stay.

"We'll wait for you out front by the changing rooms," Caroline said.

"Sounds good," Tommy said.

Gabe and Caroline waded out of the water, dragging their inner tubes onto the beach, and deposited them at the drop off spot to be handed out to the next group of visitors.

They walked to the locker room. Gabe went inside and gathered up his and Caroline's belongings leaving the cousins' stuff in the locker.

He came out, handed Caroline the day bag containing her shoes and clothes, and they went to the changing booths to get dressed.

Ten minutes later, they found a bench and sat waiting for Tommy and Amy so Gabe could hand over the locker key so the cousins could change into their clothes.

"How's your eye?" Caroline asked.

"I'll survive," he said, rubbing his eye.

"Let me see." Caroline reached over and gently pulled Gabe's hand back so she could take a look. "It looks red. Wait," she said looking at his other eye. "They're both red."

"It's the chlorine," Gabe said, covering his eye again. "Hey, do you know what a pirate's favorite letter is?"

"No. What?"

"Arrr."

37

VISTA POINT

Rather than risk the chance of being spotted tailing the vehicle, Mack drove on by when the SUV turned off the main road and headed down a narrow drive to what appeared to be a private airstrip with two warehouse-sized hangars, more than a dozen rows of private single-engine planes, and a couple of larger twin-prop transport aircraft.

Mack pulled over to the side of the road. "What now?"

Anna glanced out the windshield and saw a dirt road that ran up a hillside to a ridge overlooking the airfield. "Maybe we can get a better look from up there."

The rental car proved suitable for most of the drive up the steep incline, though the rear tires did spin out near the top causing the vehicle to go sideways but Mack was able to regain control, goosing the accelerator as they reached the summit.

"This would make the perfect vista point," Anna said. Not only did they have a sharpshooter's view of the small airport, they were high enough to see the magnificent city of Hangshong with its dramatic skyline far off in the distance. Anna could even make out the bullet-shaped Chang Empire Building, which stood out from the rest of the architecture like a saguaro cactus on a rocky plain.

Anna and Mack got out of the car, walked over, and stood on the ridge.

"Be nice to have some binoculars," Mack said.

The SUV had pulled up to the side of one of the hangars. Four doors opened up and the men got out. It was too far to get a decent description, only that they were all dressed in black and wearing hoods.

A side door in the hangar swung open and a man stepped out. He walked up to the group of Cryptos like he had been expecting them, shaking one man's hand.

"Be nice to know what they're saying," Mack said.

"We could go down and introduce ourselves," Anna said.

"Sure, and while we're at it, we could slip them our business cards."

"We still need to go down there and see what's going on." Anna pulled her Glock 19 out of her holster, ejected the clip to make sure it was fully loaded, popped it back in the handgrip, ratcheted the slide back, and put one in the chamber.

"Maybe there's a window around back," Mack said, drawing his service weapon.

They were just about to head down the sloping hillside when they heard blaring sirens coming from the direction of the city.

"What the hell is that?" Mack said.

"Sounds like a warning system," Anna said.

The ground under their feet trembled and the rental car rocked violently on its chassis, enough to trigger the anti-theft alarm. Chunks of loose rock and clumps of dirt tumbled down the hill.

Anna stumbled backward, fighting to stay on her feet as Mack staggered toward the side of the car. She heard a loud rumble, and then a three-foot wide fissure opened up between her and Mack, threatening to swallow her partner up. "Mack, watch out!" she screamed. Mack leaped over the chasm.

Turning to the sound of the sirens coming from the far away city, Anna witnessed a tall structure snap in half like an icicle breaking off an eave. More buildings swayed and came apart. She could see heavy plumes of smoke billowing up between the collapsing high-rises.

A hard jolt knocked Anna to the ground. She looked for Mack but couldn't see him in the cloud of swirling grit. It was like being buffeted by rotary blades from a hovering helicopter.

She crawled blindly on her hands and knees, unable to see in the whirling dust as the ground buckled beneath her.

"Anna! Where are you?" Mack yelled.

Before she could answer, a large shadow came toward her.

She scrambled out of the path of the rental car as it slid over the edge and rolled sideways down the hillside, flipping over onto its roof, swept up in the rockslide piling up at the bottom of the slope.

Mack stood over Anna and helped her up. He looked out across the valley and said, "Jeez, will you look at that?"

Anna could see black smoke over the city from erupting fires.

She turned and gazed down at the rental car half buried under the rocks at the bottom of the hill. "Well, there goes our ride."

One of the hangars had collapsed on the small airfield but the one the men were in was still standing.

The SUV seemed to have escaped damage.

"Or not," she said.

38

RUMBLE

Jack and Nora were standing at the same spot where they had seen the utility cart come out from behind the shrubberies when they heard a thunderous rumble like a speeding locomotive barreling toward them. A powerful shockwave ripped beneath them like the quick snap of a wet towel.

"Holy shit, it's a monster earthquake!" Jack yelled, grabbing hold of Nora as they struggled to stay on their feet like passengers on the deck of a cruise ship pitching in a rough sea. Jack heard people shouting and women and children screaming.

Situated near the garden area between the raptor exhibit and Yeren Temple, Jack and Nora watched the devastating destruction. Heavy tiles slid off the shaking buildings and fell on park visitors, burying them under the rubble.

Jack looked up and saw the cable snap on Sky-High. A string of two-person chairs plummeted from the lift. A man and a woman fell into the fenced-in pen and the gaping mouths of the giant toads.

The sprawling branches on the humongous Jinmenju tree snapped off, crushing people as they ran for safety.

Unable to withstand the jarring shake, the walls collapsed on Fu Lion Pavilion and the roof caved in. The brickwork on a nearby watchtower began to crumble, causing the structure to fall in on itself.

Jack heard a piercing screech and looked up. A speeding train derailed on Cobra Fury and flew over their heads, burrowing into the ground like a spinning drill bit.

"Oh my God, look!" Nora pointed to the giant slides at Splash Down. The eighty-foot tall tubes were splitting apart at the seams, spilling out bathers. Support beams splashed down into the lagoon.

Jack and Nora ran past the fenced-in white deer and dashed through the garden area to the entrance of Yeren Temple, dodging people running frantically out of the building while heavy tiles shattered on the steps strewn with bodies of those struck from the bone-crushing debris.

"We have to get Lennie out of there," Nora yelled, staying close to the wall to avoid being struck by the bombarding tiles.

The giant room was filled with swirling dust. An overhead beam snapped and swung down like a pendulum, punching through the thick exhibit glass between the Xing-Xings' enclosure and Lennie's.

The one-armed monkeys had already gotten free and were fighting in the middle of the room like two feuding backwoods families.

"Look out!" Jack yelled when a fifty-pound Xing-Xing came at them. Knowing he would be no match against the powerful animal, Jack scanned the floor for a weapon and spotted a club-sized piece of splintered wood. He picked up the board, stepped back to shield Nora, and when the Xing-Xing leaped in the air, Jack thrust the sharp end into the primate's chest. The ape shrieked and crashed to the floor.

"Oh my God," Nora said, when she saw three Xing-Xings knuckle walking in their direction.

"We have to get out of here," Jack said.

Jack and Nora turned to run then realized there was nowhere for them to go.

Two Xing-Xings blocked the entrance like a pair of brawlers bracing for a fight.

39

DESPERATION

At first, Gabe thought that one of the giant pistons in the wave pool had thrown a rod when he felt the sudden jolt and the asphalt beneath them buckle suddenly, tossing Caroline and him from the park bench.

"Oh my God," Caroline screamed, landing flat on her belly.

Gabe came down next to her. "Are you okay?" he said, struggling to get on his hands and knees. It was like kneeling on a vibrating paint-mixer shaker.

He flashed on the natural disaster movie *San Andres* that he had seen in a movie theater with booming surround sound and how realistic the special visual effects seemed when the 9.6 magnitude earthquake annihilated the city of San Francisco, even causing a tidal wave. But that had been make-believe; *this was real!*

He heard the sound of grinding metal and looked up.

The Splash Down tube slides were twisting like four giant flex straws and bursting apart at the seams, spilling out bathers, many flailing their arms and legs comically, though it was no laughing matter when they belly flopped, or landed squarely on their backs in the shallow water, some missing the lagoon all together and splattering on the concrete support foundations.

"My God," Caroline shouted. "Amy and Tommy are still in there!"

Tubular chutes broke apart and came crashing down on swimmers. People were screaming hysterically, scrambling to get out of the pool, dashing onto the man-made beach, everyone running in the same direction like frantic sheep mindlessly fleeing a hungry predator.

Gabe saw the thirty-foot high perimeter wall surrounding the park give way in places, brick and mortar demolishing into ruinous heaps.

A roller coaster trestle suddenly sunk ten feet into the ground, snapping the rails, and collapsed into the wave pool pumping station. Gabe heard the horrendous sound of fallen metal striking machinery and concrete. Damaged pistons sent water surging over the abutment onto dry land, forming a three-foot tsunami, so powerful, it knocked people off their feet and sent many sprawling face-first into the swift current.

Gabe and Caroline ran perpendicular to the fast-flowing water and managed to get to higher ground near the lagoon.

Already scores of bodies were floating facedown on the surface.

Everywhere around them structures kept falling down creating thick, dust clouds while the earth continued to shake.

Twenty seconds seemed like an eternity, and then the trembling stopped.

Caroline stared out over the water and cupped her hands around her mouth, yelling, "Amy! Tommy! Can you hear me?"

Which seemed improbable with all the chaos around them.

Thousands of park visitors shouting, some helping the injured or digging with their bare hands for those buried under the rubble, many staggering around too dazed to know what had just happened. Parents protecting their children, families split apart, lost souls sitting on the ground.

While Caroline continued to call out for Amy and Tommy, Gabe reached in his pants pocket and took out his cell phone. It took him only a couple of seconds to find the right app. "You're not going to believe this."

"What?" Caroline said.

"We just had an 8.3 magnitude earthquake."

"Are you serious?"

"The epicenter was right in the middle of the city."

"Oh boy. That means we're stuck here." Caroline turned and shouted, "Amy! Where are you?"

Despite all the noise around them, Gabe heard a woman's voice answer back. "I think I hear her," he said.

It was Amy. She and Tommy were wading in waist-high water. Tommy was being brave for his cousin, pushing floating bodies out of their path so Amy wouldn't freak out.

"Thank God," Caroline said, waving to get their attention.

Gabe glanced over at the building with the dressing room. A sidewall had collapsed but the rest of the structure seemed intact. "Maybe I should go get their things from the locker room."

"Gabe! What's that?"

Something was swimming just below the surface about ten feet in front of them.

Gabe took a step forward to get a better look and was able to identify it right away. "Don't worry, it's only a fish."

"What do you mean?"

"It's one of those fish from the aquarium."

Amy finally spotted Gabe and Caroline on the abutment and called out, "Guys!"

Caroline turned to Gabe with a worried look. "Oh my God, Gabe. If the fish got out..." She faced the water and screamed, "Amy! Tommy! Get out of there! Now!"

Gabe waved them on. "Get out of the water!"

Tommy trudged through the water, cupping his hands to propel himself forward.

Amy was having trouble keeping up and trailed a few feet behind; enough space for a dead woman—with the back of her skull missing—to float in between them.

"Tommy, help!" Amy screamed.

But before Tommy could go back for her, an enormous twenty-foot long shape knifed through the water and came up behind Amy.

The giant Guai Wu exploded out of the water like a blue whale executing a barrel roll and splashed down on top of Amy, taking her down with it.

"No, no!" Tommy screamed.

"Get out of there, Tommy!" Caroline yelled.

Another Guai Wu—or maybe it was the same one—lurched out of the water, grabbing Tommy with its flipper arms and pulled him under the surface.

Gabe saw more of the seal-like creatures converge on the rippling circle where Tommy had disappeared. Turbulent gouts of blood bubbled to the surface.

"Oh my God, no!" Caroline screamed.

"Son of a bitch!" Gabe yelled. He put his arm around Caroline and turned her away, knowing there was nothing they could do to save them. He felt doubly bad knowing that if he had been adamant about keeping his plans to take Caroline to his parents for spring break and maybe talked Amy into convincing her father to find a way to get his money back after booking their trip, Amy and Tommy would still be alive and not bloody chum at the bottom of the lagoon. "What do we do now?"

Caroline was crying. "I don't..." She brushed her cheek. "Wait a minute. I know someone who might help us."

"Who?"

"The FBI agents that were on our flight."

"Yeah? But how are you going to reach them?"

"Agent Rivers gave me her card. I have it somewhere," Caroline said, and began digging through her purse.

40

BLACK MARKET

Climbing down the gravely slope was like dancing on marbles. Twice, Mack fell and slid down on his butt, ruining the seat of his slacks and scuffing up his shoes. Each time he went down, Anna—who had the grace and agility of a gazelle—couldn't help but laugh. She loved ribbing him every chance she got: even in the worst predicaments.

Upon reaching the bottom, Anna and Mack stayed low and crept across the tarmac to the black SUV parked outside the hangar.

Luckily, no one was guarding the vehicle.

Mack peered through the driver's window. "We're in luck. They left the fob in the cup holder." He was about to reach for the door handle when Anna shook her head.

"Not yet," she said. "We still need to know what they're doing in there. Let's go around back."

The still-standing hangar was long enough to house a commercial airliner. They went past the single door on the side where Mack and Anna had seen the man come out to greet the Cryptos when they had arrived. It wasn't until the agents rounded the corner to the backside of the hangar that they saw two sets of windows. They crept over to the first window and raised their heads slowly to gaze inside.

The room was set up like an office with a desk and chair, two couches against opposite walls, and a few filing cabinets. A door was partially open but offered no real view of what was going on inside the hangar.

Anna and Mack moved to the next window.

From there, they could see men working diligently, staging wheeled carts, some with animal cages, others with three-foot tall saplings in black plastic five-gallon pots, next to the open loading bay of a cargo jetliner.

Anna spotted the Cryptos in their hooded sweatshirts and balaclavas, all carrying Uzi submachine guns, watching in what appeared to be a supervisory capacity while men in tanned uniforms did the actual work.

A man holding a clipboard gazed down into one of the cages on a cart, made a notation, and then said something to the worker.

"Recognize him?" Anna whispered to Mack.

"Well if it isn't Dr. Haun Zhang. What's he doing here?"

"No good by the looks of things."

"What do you think are in those cages? And what's with the nursery trees?"

Anna took out her cell phone. "Maybe I can get a clear picture." She held up her phone and clicked off a few random shots. Ducking down, she scrolled to the first clear image, and tapped her finger on the glass to enlarge the photos. Anna held up the screen so Mack could get a good look at the cartful of saplings.

"They're fruit trees, so what?" Mack said.

Anna shrugged and went to the next picture. "Take a look."

Mack studied the animal in the cage, and then said, "That's a lion cub."

"Try again," Anna said, enlarging the screen even further. "That's a Fu Lion."

"Zhang must be head of some kind of smuggling ring."

"And as the Cryptos are here, we can tie Wilde to their shady little operation."

"Nail two creeps with one rock," Mack said. "I like it. Think Chang is involved?"

"No idea. Come on, let's—" Anna's ringer shrilled on her phone.

"Jesus, Anna." Mack stuck his head up to make sure no one heard from inside the hangar while Anna fumbled to silence her phone.

Two Cryptos were staring back at him.

"We've got to get out of here!"

Anna and Mack bolted around the corner and sprinted toward the SUV.

The side door of the hangar opened the second Mack reached the driver-side door.

The men in hoods and masks stormed out. One of them cut loose with a steady barrage just as Mack flung open the door and jumped behind the steering wheel. Bullets pinged off the rear bumper and punched holes in the fender, a few taking out the rear side window.

An angry voice yelled, "You stupid idiot, that's our ride."

Anna crawled in the passenger side and shut the door. "Drive, drive!"

Mack stepped on the brake pedal and pushed the start button, slammed it into gear, and stomped on the accelerator, all the time keeping his head down as he gunned the getaway vehicle away from the airfield. He glanced over at his partner and saw Anna staring at her phone. "Who almost got us killed?"

"I'm not sure. I don't recognize the number." Anna hit redial. "Hello, who is this?"

"Hello, hello, can you hear me?" a panicked voice came on the phone. "This is Caroline Rollins."

"Caroline?" Anna glanced over at Mack. "It's the senator's daughter."

"Is she okay?" Mack asked, keeping his eyes on the road.

"Are you hurt?"

"No," Caroline replied. "But our friends are dead."

"I'm so sorry," Anna said. "Who is with you?"

"My boyfriend. Gabe. Gabe Wells."

"He wouldn't by any chance be Nick Wells' son?"

"Why, yes. How did you know?" Caroline said.

"Mack and I were assigned to look after his parents when they were in D.C."

"Oh my God. Really?"

"Where are you?"

"We're at the park."

"What park?"

"Cryptid Kingdom."

"Call me back when you find a safe place and we'll come and get you."

"All right. I have to warn you, it's pretty crazy here."

"Not half as crazy as out here," Anna said. "We're on our way."

41

TEMPLE OF MONKEYS

As soon as Nora and Jack realized they were trapped and were unable to exit Yeren Temple because of the two savage Xing-Xings blocking the doorway to the outside, they decided it was best to remain calm and not panic, even though the other three fifty-pound apes were only twenty feet away; agitated having seen Jack kill one of their own. The dead ape was on the floor with the shaft of wood protruding from its chest.

Nora knew if they tried to run, the primates would sense their fear and attack. The baboon-sized apes showed their yellow teeth and snarled, posturing to get up the nerve to avenge their dead comrade.

The Yibimins hadn't stopped fighting since they had escaped from their enclosure and were flogging each other so viciously, that three were already dead. The one-armed monkeys, deceased on the floor, were so battered they resembled nothing more than mangled, bloody lumps of fur. The remaining left-arm Yibimins continued to screech and throttle the shrieking right-arm cryptids.

If anything, the manic monkeys were a much-needed distraction, as the only alternative for Nora and Jack was to retreat deeper inside the Temple in hopes of distancing themselves from the unpredictable Xing-Xings, who at the moment were grunting and pounding the floor with their fists, displaying their disdain for the annoying Yibimins.

"There should be a service door in the back," Jack whispered, staring at the apes and taking a cautious step back. "I forgot. Do we establish eye contact with these things or not?"

"Not directly," Nora said in a low voice, following Jack's lead and slowly moving away. "And whatever you do, don't smile. They see teeth and they'll think you're being aggressive."

"Don't worry, I'm not smiling."

Nora glanced over her shoulder. The dust had settled somewhat and she could see across the large room littered with rubble, and the damaged front to Lennie's enclosure.

A heavy beam had crushed much of the fake foliage.

There was no sign of Lennie.

Nora prayed he wasn't buried under the fallen debris.

Finally, the Xing-Xings had had enough of the deranged monkeys with all their noise and nonstop scrabbling. The primates charged the smaller creatures and quickly decimated the Yibimins, pummeling them with their fists and ripping the screeching monkeys apart with their teeth. The two Xing-Xings guarding the main entrance left their posts to join in on the brutal assault. Still there was no way Nora and Jack could skirt around the mayhem without fear of being attacked.

Nora saw a Xing-Xing grab a monkey by its single arm and use it like a mace ball on a chain, slamming the animal to the floor and cracking open its skull like a coconut.

"Come on," Jack said, scurrying toward the far side of the room.

The floor shook and more debris rained down.

"It's another tremor," Nora said.

A portion of the ceiling caved in. Orange tiles crashed down like they were falling out of a World War II airplane's bomb bay, many hitting the Xing-Xings like they were intended targets, killing two in the process and mortally injuring another; the Yibimins now all dead and scattered about like ambushed victims in a massacre.

Covered in dust, and angry as ever, the two remaining Xing-Xings zeroed in on Nora and Jack.

Jack searched the floor for a weapon.

The savage apes charged, loping on all fours.

"Oh my God," Nora yelled, knowing they had only seconds before...

Lennie stepped in front of Nora and Jack. He backhanded the first Xing-Xing to leap in the air and sent it flying across the room like it had been shot out of a tennis ball launcher. The second ape met its fate when Lennie used his fist and came down on its head like a mallet ringing the bell at a carnival.

Once Jack was satisfied that the Xing-Xings were no longer a threat, he gazed up at the twelve-foot tall Yeren and said, "Nice of you to join us."

Lennie puffed out his chest and rolled his shoulders forward, flexing his muscles, and then looked down at Nora. She reached up and stroked his huge hand that was twice that of a silverback gorilla. Lennie worked his thick, black lips into what could be construed as a grin.

"We better get out of here before the rest of it comes down," Jack said.

"Let's hope it's safer out there," Nora said.

They stepped through the wreckage and over the dead creatures, and went outside.

Most of the buildings she could see looked like a wrecking ball had demolished them; even sections of the wall surrounding the 100-acre park had sustained damage from the quake.

Hundreds of people were climbing over the rubble, trying to find a way out of the ruination.

Lennie let out a deep-throated growl.

"What is it, Len?" Nora said, gazing up at the scowling Yeren and then turning to see what he was looking at.

Instant panic gripped the pit of her stomach like a clenched fist.

A Fu Lion was roaming through the scraps of lumber and piles of ruin, searching for food as another Fu Lion in the background was feeding on what looked to be a man's body. Nora saw partially eaten corpses lying everywhere, perhaps left intentionally to be snacked upon for later meals.

Both Fu Lions looked up, catching the scent of new prey, and glared at Nora, Jack, and Lennie.

42

SEWER RATS

Finder feared they would be buried alive when the passageway suddenly shuddered and huge cracks opened up in the ceiling and heavy chunks of cement came crashing down all around them. The overhead lights went out as they tried to outrun the falling debris, trapping them in the dark.

Then the red emergency lights came on, transforming the blinding dust into a suffocating crimson fog.

"We have to go back for my father," Luan shouted, covering her mouth with her hand as she struggled to breathe. Her face was smudged, her black hair gray from the soot in the air. Her clothes were so filthy; she looked like she had been crawling through the desert for days.

Finder glanced back and saw the tunnel sealed by tons of concrete boulders. "I'm afraid that's not possible! We'll have to find another way!"

The tunnel ahead gave way in a tumultuous roar. Finder grabbed Luan by the arm and they fled down a side corridor, chased by a raging cloud of billowing dust.

They kept running and quickly reached the main concourse of the underground facility where workers were scrambling to avoid being struck by the hailing debris.

"What's the best way out of here?" Finder asked Luan.

Luan looked down the rows of employees' shops and the series of glass entrances leading to the workers' living quarters. She turned to her right and pointed down a wide passageway. "There should be a service stairwell that way."

"Let's hope it isn't blocked off," Finder said.

They were about to start down the thoroughfare when Finder heard a groundbreaking roar like a dam giving way and then the onslaught of rushing water.

Before Finder and Luan could even think to turn the other way and run, the flood was upon them, scooping them off their feet, and plunging them into the torrential four-foot deep watercourse.

The ceiling cracked open and people in bathing suits cascaded down like trout spilling over a waterfall. Finder figured they were drowning victims from the water park.

Bodies slammed into them as Finder and Luan fought to keep their heads above the surface. The fast-flowing river propelled them to the center of the concourse where the floodwater flattened out and dispersed into shallower areas of standing water.

"Are you hurt?" Finder asked Luan. He waded over and helped her up.

They stood knee-deep in the water amongst fifty or more bloated bathers that looked like so many dead fish washed up on a beach after a storm.

Finder heard a buildup of loud screeches coming in their direction. "What the hell is that?"

A flotilla of large furry creatures was dogpaddling towards them. Finder took one hard look. "My God, tell me those aren't what I think they are."

"Yes, they are rats," Luan confirmed. "Bamboo rats."

The Goddamn things are huge! Finder thought to himself. They looked more like giant beavers. Seeing them swimming on the surface, Finder guessed each one had to weigh in the vicinity of 80 pounds—and there were more than a hundred rats.

"Where's that exit again?" Finder asked.

The giant rodents split up and swam for the floating bodies. As there were more rats than people, two or more would set upon a single body, ripping out chunks of flesh with their sharp teeth and claws, many unwilling to share and fighting amongst themselves.

Finder saw a rat swimming straight for Luan. "Look out!" he yelled, trying to kick the rat's head but only able to splash it with water.

The tip of a metal pole plunged into the rat's back and made a crackling sound, causing the rodent to squeal.

Finder saw the burn patch on its fur then looked up at the woman holding a stock prod with two electrodes on the end. The rat she had given the high-voltage to was already scampering through the water to get away.

Luan turned to the woman. "Song, thank God."

"Come Dr. Chang, we must go this way," Song Liu instructed.

Finder let Luan and Song go ahead of him so he could make sure the rats didn't follow but then realized there was no reason to worry as the rats had found themselves quite the smorgasbord feasting on the floating bodies. He caught up quickly and overheard the women speaking. "Where are we going?" he asked.

"Song is concerned about a friend," Luan said, as they waded through the water.

"Why, what happened?"

"She believes he is in trouble. She thinks you may know him."

"Who is he?" Finder asked.

Luan said, "Song says his name is Mason. Lyle Mason."

"I don't know him," Finder replied.

Song turned to Finder. "He came here with the others. He works for you."

"If he came here with the cryptids, then he must be one of Dr. McCabe's men as I certainly never met him."

"Will you help me? Find Mason," Song said desperately.

"Sure. We'll help. Where's the last place you saw him?"

"I'll show you."

They sloshed their way through the water and stopped when they reached a convex concrete wall with a metal door.

"He was right here," Song said. "The door is locked. Only Dr. Zhang can open it."

"And me," Luan said. "I have a master keycard." Luan took out her card and swiped it inside the reader on the wall. The lock made a mechanical click and the door popped open. Luan stepped inside and the lights automatically came on.

A naked man was lying on the floor.

"Oh my God. It is Mason," Song said.

"Is he alive?" Finder asked Luan as she felt Mason's neck for a pulse.

"Yes. Help me sit him up."

Finder hoisted Mason up by the shoulders and propped him up while Luan tried to wake him up by gently slapping the side of his face.

Mason's eyes fluttered. "Hey...what...the..."

"What happened to you?" Finder asked.

"I don't know," Mason said groggily.

"Look what I found," Song said. She held up a used syringe and an empty vial.

"What does the label on the bottle say?" Luan asked.

"Vecuronium bromide."

"What the hell is that?" Mason said.

"It's used to paralyze muscles on patients during surgery," Luan said.

"Hey, where are my clothes?"

"Right here." Luan found Mason's clothes neatly stacked on a table, along with his boots.

Song turned her back to give Mason a moment to get dressed. Finder and Luan went over to gaze through the small window at the dark room on the other side of the wall.

"What's in there?" Finder asked.

"The rooting system for the Jinmenju tree," Luan said.

Finder noticed the pull-down door on the wall. He yanked down the handle, peered down the chute, and got a good whiff. "Smells like a compost pile of rotten fruit."

Song flicked on a wall switch and the lights came on in the room.

"Oh my God," Luan said, staring through the window. "There's something moving in the dirt."

Mason staggered over and squeezed between Finder and Luan so he could get a look. "You got to be shitting me," Mason said.

Tentacle-like roots were slithering about the loose dirt in search of nourishment.

Mason looked at Finder and Luan, and then at Song. "Damn bastard was going to feed me to that thing! He must have done the same to Ramsey. Son of a bitch!"

43

DR. ZHANG'S ZANY LAB

Every muscle in Mason's body ached and his head throbbed. He feared he might throw up at any moment from the after-effects of the drug. But still, he was able to keep up with the others—doing his best to ignore the stench—as they waded through the floodwaters log-jammed with bobbing bodies.

"What's happened here?" Mason said, thinking they looked like victims from a shipwreck.

"You didn't feel it?" Finder said.

"Feel what?"

"The earthquake."

"Hell no!"

"Dr. Zhang must have put you under before it struck," Luan said.

"Lucky me," Mason said sarcastically.

"I am glad you are all right," Song said, holding onto Mason's arm and helping him along.

"Too bad we can't say the same for Ramsey. So, do you think this Dr. Zhang is still around?" Mason asked.

"If he is, he might be in his laboratory or in his living quarters," Luan said.

"Wait till I get my hands on him!"

"Steady there," Finder said. "We find him, I'll make sure he pays for what he's done."

"Here we are." Luan used her keycard and opened the glass entrance to a small foyer with two doors. She ran her card down the reader, opening the door on the left.

Finder was first to enter Dr. Zhang's living quarters.

Mason followed and thought the accommodations were a step up from the private room he had been sharing with Ramsey but not by much. The women came in after him but didn't venture too far inside.

Finder walked into the bedchamber and quickly came out. "He's not here."

"Perhaps he is in his laboratory," Luan said.

Everyone went back into the vestibule and waited while Luna swiped her card to open the other door.

As soon as they went in, Finder said, "Do you smell that? It's the same smell as that tree."

The laboratory was a fair size, maybe twenty by thirty feet. High-powered microscopes, spectrometers, Bunsen burners, racks of test tubes, and other laboratory instruments a scientist would expect to use, occupied three rows of workbenches.

Mason watched Luan scan the laboratory with a critical eye like an OSHA safety inspector searching for violations. "Do you work with Dr. Zhang?" he asked.

"No," Luan said, bending forward to peer in a microscope eyepiece. "I have never been inside this lab. Dr. Zhang is very protective of his research."

"I think you should look at this," Finder called out.

Mason and the women walked by the workbenches—the strange smell becoming stronger—and found Finder behind a partition, standing at the end of a large wooden table with twenty-four potted saplings in five-gallon containers.

"What's he doing back here; growing Bonsai trees?" But then Mason noticed the clear plastic tubing with a red liquid flowing within, set up like an irrigation drip system, each pot with a separate tube inserted in the soil.

Luan went over to the other side of the table and followed the feeder lines that were attached to portals on a stainless-steel container that looked like a refrigerator on its back. She opened the lid and looked inside. "Oh my God. He's got it stocked with liter bags of plasma and blood."

It reminded Mason of a similar scene from the movie *The Thing from Another World* when the scientists were using seeds to create new life—hanging on plasma bag holders and pulsating like pairs of lungs—harvested from the alien invader's severed arm.

Mason put his palms on the table and leaned over to take a closer look at one of the trees. "What's this?" he said, and picked what looked like a tiny berry. He held it between his thumb and forefinger and squeezed: bursting it like a bloated mosquito filled with blood.

"Funny," Luan said. "Dr. Zhang never mentioned he was attempting to grow more Jinmenju trees."

"There's probably a lot of things he isn't telling you," Finder said, having opened a storage locker. He reached in and took out a backpack. He unzipped the bag and dumped the contents onto the floor. Out fell some textbooks and a small clutch purse with a few odds and ends. He picked up the purse, looked inside, and found a student ID card.

Song opened another locker. She found two daypacks stacked on top of one another. Mason tried the next locker and discovered two more.

"Oh my God," Luan said. "The rumors were true."

"What rumors?" Finder asked.

"It was never proven but Dr. Zhang was suspected of abducting and killing some of his students."

"He probably hung them on his damn tree," Mason said venomously.

Luan broke into tears.

"What is it?" Finder asked.

"It means my father has known about Dr. Zhang for all these years," Luan said in between sobs.

"That is not all," Song said. "Look at this."

Mason turned and saw Song pointing to two rectangular tables, each with double rows of what appeared to be ten-gallon fish tanks. He could hear a steady hum coming from a machine.

Each glass container had a single occupant, suspended in a dank liquid. "What is that? Formaldehyde?" Mason asked.

One of the specimens moved. "Holy shit," he said. "They're alive?"

Luan approached the tanks. "Yes. They are fetuses. The liquid you see must be a synthetic embryonic fluid. You will notice that they all have umbilical cords and are hooked up to that machine."

"What are they?" Mason asked.

Finder and Song moved around the tanks to get a better look at the fetuses.

"Fu Lions," Luan said.

"How many of these creatures were you planning to have in the park?" Mason asked.

"Only the two we currently have," Luan said.

"Looks like the doctor has plans of his own," Mason said.

44

A FALLING OUT

Carter Wilde woke up disoriented, half buried in rumble. He had no idea how long he had been unconscious. The last thing he remembered was the walls shaking and the watchtower crumbling all around him. He was able to raise his left arm and clear off some of the debris, enough that he could sit up. He felt the back of his head. His scalp was sticky, and when he looked at his hand, his fingertips were covered with blood.

He gazed around the demolished room that earlier was a prestigious box seat and saw a body lying at the base of the bar covered with fallen debris. Wilde managed to get on his feet and stumbled across the uneven rubble. He looked down at the man covered in grime. "Joel, how bad is it?"

Dr. McCabe made a face. "My arm's broken," his voice was wheezy. "Maybe some ribs."

Wilde, too, was having trouble breathing, and for a surreal moment, thought he was sharing a symbiotic experience of empathy with his brother. But then Wilde inhaled and choked on the thick brick dust in the air and knew that was the real reason for his shortness of breath.

Dropping to one knee, Wilde said, "Hang on," and rummaged through his coat pocket but came up empty. He glanced about, hoping to spot his cell phone.

He saw Henry Chang's legs sticking out from under a crossbeam lying across his chest, his right arm penned—possibly severed—under the twisted steel. Chang attempted to move and let out a mournful cry.

Wilde heard bricks tumble down behind him. He turned and saw one of his bodyguards—Simmons or was it Shelton, he couldn't quite remember—climbing down through an unstable hole in the wall.

"Sir, are you hurt?" asked the bodyguard.

"No. Help Dr. McCabe," Wilde said.

The burly bodyguard stomped over. He reached down to grab McCabe by both hands.

"Not the arm," Dr. McCabe said.

"Are you able to walk?" Wilde asked McCabe as the bodyguard gingerly helped the doctor to his feet.

"Sure, I'm..." but when he took a step, McCabe collapsed. The bodyguard caught him, slipped his arm under McCabe's armpit, and reached around the doctor's back to keep him on his feet.

"Help me," Chang pleaded. A spurt of blood squirted out from under the beam.

Wilde came over and stood over Chang. "How much?"

"What?" Chang said, wincing with pain.

"How much is it worth to you for my help?" Wilde asked snidely. "Certainly we can do better than twenty percent."

"All right, all right," Chang grimaced. "I will give you thirty percent of the franchise."

"Goodbye Henry."

"No, no stop. Forty."

"I'm sure you can do better than that," Wilde said.

"Tell him you want the patents to his daughter's work," McCabe said.

Chang glared up at Wilde. "I will not!"

"Sounds fair to me," Wilde said. "Especially after the way you disrespected me."

"What about Dr. Zhang?" Chang said.

"What about him?"

"You can have his biological patents. Now please, I need medical attention."

"What makes you think he'll just hand them over?" Wilde asked.

"Because I know what he did and I own them," Chang replied.

"What, you're blackmailing Zhang?"

"Just as long as Dr. Zhang works for me," Chang said, "his secrets will be safe."

"Well, I hate to burst your bubble, but your Dr. Zhang now works for me. Oh, and that forty percent. Not interested."

"Damn you, Wilde! I will ruin you!"

"I really don't think you are in any position to make threats." Wilde turned to his bodyguard assisting McCabe. "Here, let me take him." He went over and supported his brother.

"Do you want me to go get help?" the bodyguard asked.

"No!" Wilde said adamantly. "I want you to put Mr. Chang out of his misery."

"Carter, are you sure?" McCabe said. "It could make trouble for us."

"Wilde, you son of a bitch!" Chang screamed.

The bodyguard stepped up to Chang and pulled his gun out from under his suit jacket. He pointed the muzzle at Chang's head.

"No, you moron," Wilde said.

The bodyguard turned to his boss.

"It has to look like he died from the earthquake."

Holstering his gun, the bodyguard searched around, and picked up a large hunk of concrete the size of a bowling ball.

"That's more like it," Wilde said.

The bodyguard raised the cement chunk over his head.

Everyone froze to the sudden chatter of Chinese on the other side of the high mound of broken bricks.

Not knowing what they were saying, Wilde didn't know if they were frightened visitors scrambling for a way out, a rescue team searching for survivors, or Chang's men looking for their employer.

"Shit, forget it. Let's go!" Wilde said.

The bodyguard dropped the intended murder weapon.

Wilde and the big man helped McCabe through a gap in the wall onto the parapet walkway and hurried as fast as they could, leaving the clamoring voices behind.

45

8-HEADED BEAST

"Watch it!" Anna yelled when another car cut in front of them. Mack swerved to miss the oncoming vehicle speeding out of Cryptid Kingdom's chaotic parking lot.

Hundreds of people ran frantically between the parked cars. They had to dodge automobiles ramming into other vehicles as though they were spectators that had mistakenly stepped into the middle of a track at a demolition derby.

Anna cringed when she saw a man get mowed down, and the car that struck him ran over his body, the front tire rolling over his head, and the rear finishing off the job, flattening his gourd onto the asphalt.

The lane was blocked up ahead by a three-car wreck.

"It's no use," Mack said. "We're going to have to chance it on foot."

Getting out her side, Anna heard screaming and the constant slamming of metal on metal as more cars careened into one another.

A woman and three children ran toward her. Anna sidestepped to let them pass.

The youngest girl trailing behind tripped and fell on the ground.

Anna rushed over and helped her up. "Are you hurt, sweetie?" She couldn't have been older than ten. The girl looked up at Anna, her eyes wide with fear.

The mother scrambled back, screaming in Chinese. She grabbed her daughter, gave Anna a brief nod of thanks, and raced after her other children.

"Come on, I think we can get in at the southern entrance," Mack said, pulling Anna onto her feet and sprinting between the cars and the fleeing park visitors.

It took them a few minutes before they were able to reach the dragonhead archway only to find that is was blocked by twisted wrought iron and a barrier of tumbledown masonry.

"Feel up to a little wall climbing?" Mack asked.

"Lead the way," Anna replied, always up for a challenge. She watched Mack attack the dangerous pile of rubble and make it up ten feet before following him up. One false move and the entire mountain of bricks could come tumbling down in a bone-breaking avalanche. Twice, Mack slipped, dislodging a brick (each time narrowly missing his partner), still managing his ascent without sending the rest crashing down on Anna's head.

Reaching the top, they carefully descended down the other side.

Anna took out her phone and called Caroline's number. "Hello? Yes, we're here. Where are you?" She listened for a moment then ended the call.

"Well?" Mack asked.

"She said there's a lot of flooding where they're at and they're cutting across the park toward the west entrance," Anna said.

"That's good," Mack said. "We can meet them in the middle."

Anna and Mack started out and jogged beneath the trestles supporting the roller coaster track that looped around the inside perimeter of the park. A portion of the track had buckled and broken away, undermined by the earthquake, resulting in a derailed train that was upside down on the ground, surrounded by scattered bodies.

A small group of people rushed by like shell-shocked city dwellers after an air raid followed by a mixed herd of white deer with huge antlers and smaller brown deer with strange looking fangs.

"That was weird," Mack said.

"Oh yeah? Check that out," Anna said and pointed to the pack of raptors coming straight for them. Just like the deer, the bird-like dinosaurs varied in appearance, some the size of turkeys with blue and red feathers, the others as big as ostriches covered with green plumes.

Unsure if they were an immediate threat, Anna and Mack drew their side arms.

Two of the larger dinosaurs headed in their direction. Mack raised his gun and fired a shot in the air.

The raptors turned abruptly and darted toward the ruins of a building that had completely collapsed next to a sign: DRAGON PAGODA.

Anna saw the uppermost part of the rubble bulge like the bubbling crust of an oven-baked potpie.

A dragon's head emerged, then another head on the end of a long neck, followed by more, until there were eight flailing heads, as one neck was missing a head. The beast pushed its body out of the rubble. It climbed out on four legs, swooshing its long tail.

"Where's a dragon slayer when you need one?" Mack quipped.

Anna aimed her gun at the beast but it was impossible to get a clear headshot with the necks thrashing about like writhing octopus tentacles. She doubted if their bullets would even penetrate its thick, scaly chest.

The 8-headed dragon lumbered down out of the wreckage like a scene straight out of a low-budget creature feature motion picture and stomped toward Anna and Mack.

"What do we do now?" Mack said.

"I've got an idea," Anna replied.

"What?"

"Run!"

46

FOWL PLAY

The Fu Lions looked like bronze statues that had suddenly come to life. Their rust-colored mullet-like manes were swirling curls stretching over their furrowed brows above flat pug noses with flaring nostrils. The sharp tips of the upper and lower incisors were visibly touching in their savage mouths that ran along the jawbones. Dangling off their chins were Fu Manchu extensions that hung down to their chests.

They were unbelievably muscular and wore ornate bridles draped around their bulging shoulders. Padlock lockets hung over their barrel chests. Armored sleeves covered their powerful legs and the talons on their two-knuckle paws were as big as railroad spikes.

The closest Fu Lion stood twenty feet away from Jack, Nora, and Lennie; the second creature twice the distance but steadily approaching.

"They're enormous," Jack said. It was impossible to guess their weight given their dense body mass. He wouldn't have been a bit surprised to learn they were pumped up on steroids.

"How are we going to get out of this one?" Nora asked, standing on Jack's right.

Jack glanced quickly over his shoulder for somewhere to retreat. The only place he could see to go was back inside the partially standing temple, but that would only mean getting cornered with nowhere to run.

"What do you think, you big oaf?" Jack said, looking up at Lennie.

"Really, Jack?" Nora said. "You're taking your playbook from him?"

Lennie stared out at the two Fu Lions and growled, baring his tombstone teeth. He even went as far as thumping his chest with his basketball-sized fist.

The Fu Lions accepted the challenge and roared back.

Jack watched the twelve-foot tall Yeren bend down and pick up a large rock.

"Seriously?" Jack said.

Lennie ignored Jack, reared back his arm, and flung the heavy rock.

Jack watched with astonishment as the rock—sounding like a hammer striking the inside of a church bell—grazed the nearest Fu Lion's shoulder.

The Fu Lion stood unfazed.

"Told you," Jack said.

Lennie reached down and picked up an even bigger rock. He hefted it in the palm of his hand like a shot-putter ready to outdistance an opponent.

"Oh, what the hell." Nora grabbed a rock off the ground.

Jack looked at her. "You'd have better luck stopping an armored truck with a water balloon."

"You have another plan, I'm all ears?" Nora said, tossing the rock like a baseball back and forth between her hands. "At least maybe we can drive them away."

"You really think it's going to work?"

"Being a cryptozoologist, I think I know a thing or two about animal behavior."

Lennie let out a fierce growl.

Jack glanced back at the Fu Lions. The nearest was standing its ground but the other Fu Lion had turned its attention to a small group of people that had the misfortune to run out from behind a hillock of rubble into the creature's domain.

The terrified park visitors saw the beast and scattered in all directions when the Fu Lion took chase.

That left only the one Fu Lion.

"Batter up, boys," Nora shouted. She threw her rock but it fell short.

Jack grabbed two decent sized rocks, wound up, and let loose with what he considered a decent fastball with a little too much assertion, as the rock flew over the Fu Lion's head. His second attempt landed to the left.

Lennie had better success and hit the Fu Lion squarely in the face with a jagged chunk of concrete.

The stone burst apart in a thousand gravelly pieces like a sledgehammer had pulverized it. Again, the Fu Lion was unfazed.

"I'm sorry, Nora, but I hardly think this is working," Jack said. He looked up at Lennie, expecting him to come up with a solution but the Yeren was just as baffled.

Jack heard what sounded like heavy machinery parts clanking together. He turned and saw the armor-wearing Fu Lion bounding towards them.

There was nothing they could do to stop it.

And then a strange bird fluttered down and landed in front of the Fu Lion.

It was the size of a pelican but instead of a pointy beak, its head was long like a horse. The fowl had a dragon-like body with reddish plates alternating with black ones down to its tapered tail. The most unusual thing about the bird were its wings, as each one looked as though they had been stripped to the bone, leaving see-through gaps, the only feathers left remaining on the outer tips.

The Fu Lion considered the bird for a moment, then in one enormous bite, gobbled up the bird whole and swallowed it down.

"Jesus, did you see that?" Jack said.

"Sure did," Nora said and smiled at Jack.

"Why are you smiling? We're next."

"I don't think so. Watch."

The Fu Lion frothed at the mouth and collapsed on the ground. "What the hell?" Jack said. "Don't tell me it choked on that bird?"

"That was a Zhenniao," Nora said. "Their feathers are extremely poisonous."

Jack looked up at Lennie. "And here I thought you gave it a concussion."

Lennie shrugged his shoulders and huffed.

47

NO LAUGHING MATTER

Anna had never run away from a fight in her entire life. She had stood toe-to-toe with the best of them, through her grueling training to become an FBI agent, to hunting down some of the most dangerous criminals on the planet. But she had the good sense to know when a situation warranted a pass. Such as when confronted by an eight-headed dragon.

Thank God it hadn't been a fire breather.

"Is it still after us?" Mack said, sprinting down a clear path between two demolished buildings.

Anna glanced back. "No. I don't see it." She slowed down to a walk, listening for the legendary creature, but no longer heard it. "I think we're good."

"Get a load of this," Mack said. "Looks like a twister tore through here."

Mack was referring to the damage done to the massive tree in the enormous granite planter in the middle of the promenade. Many of the giant branches had snapped clear off during the quake and were lying all around the perimeter of the fifteen-foot diameter trunk.

Anna saw arms and legs sticking out from under the split timber, boughs haphazardly strewn about and piled together like flood-swept detritus collected at the bottom of a washed-out ravine.

And then she heard a cackle.

"What was that?" Mack said.

Crazed laughter erupted around them.

"Sounds like someone got hit on the noggin," Anna said.

"Either that or a bunch of nut jobs escaped the loony bin."

Anna and Mack approached a fallen branch where someone underneath was giggling like they were being tickled with a feather.

Mack reached down and pulled back a leafy branch. "Holy shit!" he yelled and jumped back. "It's a frigging head."

Or rather, it was a melon-sized fruit with human facial features; and it was laughing its proverbial ass off as though it had heard the funniest joke of all time. And it wasn't alone. Anna spotted more of them; chortling and guffawing like decapitated zanies in a mental institution straight out of a horror movie.

"What is this?" Mack said. "Comedy Central?"

Anna was beginning to think the laughing heads were malfunctioning animatronics when she spotted one that looked familiar. On a lark, she took out her cell phone and began browsing pictures she had posted on her worksite.

"Mack, come here," Anna said. "You've got to see this."

Her partner waltzed over. Anna held up her phone so he could see the screen.

"Yeah, so?" Mack said.

"Take a good look." She pointed at the laughing head on the ground.

"You've got to be kidding me," Mack said. "That's the congressman's son."

"Sure is. We found Rong Tran. In a matter of speaking."

"How in the hell are we going to explain this?"

"*I* have no idea," Anna replied.

48

COME TOGETHER

Gabe and Caroline were near the rendezvous point to meet up with agents Hunter and Rivers when a CAIC Z-10 military attack helicopter swooped down over the park, the aircraft heavily armed with twin turret 30mm machine guns, a 14.5mm Gatling gun on the bow of the cockpit, two 25mm M242 Bushmaster cannons, and anti-tank missiles housed in four pods mounted beneath the two stub wings.

"Cover your head," Gabe hollered to be heard over the thunderous roar. He grabbed Caroline to shield her from the blinding dust created by the low flying war machine's swirling rotary blades. The Chinese chopper soared over the far wall of the park, banked to the left, and disappeared from sight in the twilight sky.

"That was scary," Caroline said, rubbing the grit from her face. "They're actually sending in the military?"

"Probably to assist in the rescue effort. I doubt they'd be using any deadly force with all the civilians running around." He looked to see if the helicopter was coming back and was relieved when it didn't appear that it was.

He saw a black, smoky haze on the horizon in the dusk-approaching sky. "The city must have been hit pretty hard. The airport, too."

"Meaning we'll be stranded here," Caroline said.

"We'll worry about that later." Gabe was getting his bearings when he felt the ground vibrate below his feet. "No, not another one," Gabe said, anticipating an aftershock. Often the aftershocks could be just as damaging as the initial earthquake. He heard a rumbling noise and turned, wishing it were another tremor they were experiencing instead of the ground-shaking monster coming toward them.

The Wuhnan Toad was as big as a dump truck and was next to a high pile of debris. It was so rotund, that when it leaped forward, it could only cover a distance of ten feet before landing back on the ground. The white throat sack billowed outward as it took in a deep breath.

Gabe saw its hideous mouth open suddenly. He yelled out a warning to Caroline, "Get down," the split second the albino amphibian flicked out its tongue.

The sticky tip of the elongated tongue wrapped around Caroline's waist like a fire hose and hoisted her off her feet. Gabe dove for her legs and grabbed around her knees to serve as an anchor.

Normally the tongue would have snapped back like an overstretched rubber band, but with the burden of Gabe's added weight, the toad was struggling to retract its tongue back into its mouth.

"Don't let go," Caroline pleaded.

Digging his feet into the ground, Gabe could feel his grip slipping, and knew he was on the losing end of the tug-of-war as Caroline was drawn steadily closer to the giant toad's gaping mouth, like a prize fish being slowly reeled in by a determined angler.

Caroline screamed and kept screaming, each time the pitch of her voice edging an octave higher.

* * *

"You're sure it's dead?" Jack said as they approached the Fu Lion lying facedown.

"Pretty sure," Nora said.

"Pretty sure?" Jack hesitated before taking another step. He looked up at Lennie to see if he was sharing the same trepidation. The giant Yeren's demeanor was as it always was: oafish and dullish; not to mention being besmirched. His face and massive leathery chest were no longer black, but a dusted gray from the swirling soot, and his thick orangey coat was so filthy, he looked like a wild animal that had narrowly escaped having run for its life through a raging forest fire.

Nora said, "You saw how it keeled over."

"You sure it didn't just choke on that bird?" Jack said.

"No, it was the feathers. The toxicity must be off the charts."

"Thank God for that." Jack gazed across the park and saw the crest of the sun disappearing behind the western wall like a gold piece dropping into a coin slot.

An ominous purple bruised the darkening sky; the veiling evening looming shadows everywhere.

Jack saw a quick flash in the night sky. "Jesus, did you see that? Don't tell me a storm's coming."

"That wasn't lightning," Nora said. "I'm pretty sure that was a Sky Serpent."

"What, something else we have to worry about?"

"To be honest, I don't know much about them."

Jack looked up and saw half a dozen snake-like displays of flashing light move about the darkened sky a hundred feet above their heads. "How do they stay suspended in the air like that? I don't see any wings. It's almost like a parlor trick."

"Like I said, I'm not sure."

Jack looked around and noticed that Lennie was no longer with them. "Hey, where did he take off to?"

"He was here a second ago," Nora said.

That's when they heard a woman scream.

* * *

"I can't hold on," Gabe yelled. His right hand slipped away first, then the fingers of his left hand let go. He watched in horror as the Wuhnan Toad continued to retract its tongue, dragging Caroline over the dirt.

Since the toad's tongue was attached to the front of its mouth and wasn't designed to help it swallow, it would have to wait until Caroline was completely in its mouth and then roll its eyes down into the roof of its mouth to propel a soon-to-be gluttonous meal down its throat.

Gabe scrambled to his feet and lunged to grab Caroline who was still screaming out Gabe's name, her voice becoming increasingly hoarse.

He missed her by inches and yelled, "No, no!"

A large creature stepped in front of Gabe and snatched Caroline. It looked like a Bigfoot, only twice as tall, with dirty fur and big hands. *Oh my God*, Gabe thought, *Caroline gets spared one brutal death only to suffer another?*

* * *

"It's them," Anna yelled to Mack, hearing the screams coming from the other side of a demolished building. "Caroline and Gabe."

They pulled their service pistols and ran to the edge of the wreckage.

Anna froze when she saw a huge, hairy beast lifting Caroline off the ground.

"What do we do?" Mack said. "I don't want to take a chance hitting Caroline."

"Get its attention. Maybe I can sneak up on it." Anna ran in a low crouch toward Gabe.

"Hey!" Mack shouted, waving his hands in the air. "Over here!"

The big ape turned and glared at Mack. That's when Mack saw the thick, pinkish cord wrapped around Caroline's waist.

"Agent Rivers," Gabe yelled, getting Anna's attention as she lined up a shot on the Chinese apeman. He began pointing. "Kill that, kill that!"

"What?" Anna said. She looked beyond the edge of the rubble and saw a monstrous white toad as big as a utility van.

She noticed the giant ape was holding a large rock. It came down with a powerful blow, severing the fleshy cord. Blood gushed all over Caroline and the big beast.

Once Caroline was released, she ran as fast as she could into Gabe's open arms.

Anna kept her gun trained on the big ape.

Mack climbed up the debris onto the collapsed roof. The unstable tiles beneath his feet kept shifting as he made his way to the edge.

He looked down and saw the horrendous toad. Blood speckled its face.

The toad heard Mack moving above it and looked up with its mouth wide open.

"Not today, you ugly son of a bitch!" Mack said, leaning out to take the shot. The loose tiles suddenly slid out from under him.

Mack toppled down straight into the toad's mouth, which immediately shut, having consumed a new prey.

Anna swept her gun muzzle at the gargantuan amphibian but she dared not shoot in fear of a bullet hitting her partner. That is if he were even alive.

The toad began to close its eyes, a sign that it was about to swallow.

A muffled gunshot could be heard inside the creature.

The left eyeball exploded, spraying out a clear gel, and then there was another shot and the right eye burst out of the socket like an enormous runny soft-boiled egg. A salvo of bullets exited the toad's head, punching out thin, crimson geysers.

The massive creature flopped to the ground.

Anna, Gabe, and Caroline dashed over to the dead toad.

"Mack can you hear me?" Anna shouted as they tried to pry open the creature's mouth.

"Get me out of here!" Mack answered.

Gabe and Caroline managed to prop open the mouth with their shoulders while Anna reached in and grabbed Mack's hand. She put her foot on the toad's chin and yanked, but Mack seemed to be lodged in the toad's throat. Anna could only assume that the muscles in the upper esophagus had begun to constrict in a mid-swallow to the gullet and had clamped down on her partner.

"Hurry up!" Mack shouted. "I'm suffocating in here!"

"Hold on, we're trying." A boggy stench wafted into Anna's face, a combination of organic matter being dissolved by digestive juices and hydrochloric acid at work deep within the stomach.

Brushing Anna aside, the huge apeman took over, reached inside the giant toad's mouth, and pulled Mack out.

Mack fell out onto the ground, his head and clothes covered in a mucous slime. "Thank God," he said, then saw his rescuer. He raised his gun in a knee-jerk response.

"Please, don't shoot," a woman cried out. "He won't hurt you. I promise."

Anna turned and saw a man and a woman hurrying in their direction.

"Yeah, he's just trying to help!" the man hollered.

Mack put down his gun.

"Who are you?" Anna asked, lowering her weapon.

"I'm Nora Howard and this is Jack Tremens."

"Believe it or not," Jack said, "we're here to bring Lennie home."

"This Bigfoot is yours?" Mack said.

"Technically he's a Yeren," Nora corrected Mack.

"You might say he's part of the family," Jack said, gazing up at the big ape. "Ain't that right, knucklehead?"

Lennie looked down at Jack, stuck out his fat, black tongue, and blew a wet—and extremely loud—raspberry that sounded like a flatulent bull farting into the wind.

Everyone broke out laughing.

Bricks came crashing down when a bulldozer plowed through a section of wall.

Two more heavy equipment earthmovers shoved through on their tractor treads, opening up a wider path. Scores of rescuers in red overalls and hardhats charged into the park, carrying first aid kits and folded stretchers, along with canine Search and Rescue teams. Camouflage uniformed soldiers armed with carbines came in next and dispersed quickly about the park. It wasn't long before there was sporadic gunfire.

"We have to get Lennie out of here before they shoot him," Nora said.

"This way," Anna said, pointing to a narrow opening by the west entrance. Mack ran behind Gabe and Caroline while Jack and Nora coaxed Lennie to the park exit.

49

OVER THE LINE

Carter Wilde gazed out from the hangar at the night-shrouded airfield. He was standing next to the front wheel of a Boeing 777F cargo plane that at one time had been part of the FedEx—the logo on the fuselage and the vertical stabilizer now *Wilde Enterprises*—decommissioned fleet before Wilde purchased the aircraft for a song.

"How's the arm?" Wilde asked, removing a cigar from his jacket inside pocket.

Dr. Joel McCabe's left arm was cradled in a black sling. "I'll need to have it properly set once we land." He popped the cap on a vial and swallowed a couple of pain pills.

"I'll have someone waiting," assured Wilde. "What do you think of our new venture?" The billionaire was referring to the cages upon cages of exotic creatures that were being loaded onto the plane. Four workers pushed a long glass tank on casters containing a six-foot long giant black salamander with yellow spots. The amphibian was not at all happy and kept barking and hissing, and even whining.

"Damn thing sounds like a baby," Wilde said.

"It is often called the *infant fish*."

Wilde and McCabe turned and saw Dr. Zhang approaching with his clipboard.

"You should be happy to know that samples of every cryptid that Mr. Chang had in his park are on your plane. And more." Dr. Zhang motioned to the workers pushing two animal cages toward the loading door.

"What are those?" Wilde asked.

"The white bear is a Bax-Xiong," Dr. Zhang said like a proud father, "and the brown one is a Golden Moon Bear. Very sacred."

"Well, Joel. Looks like we'll be up and running in no time," Wilde said triumphantly. "Soon we'll have parks all over the world."

"I don't think so."

Wilde turned and saw a man in a ruined suit walk into the hangar. A woman, equally disheveled, stepped in as well and stood at the man's side.

"Who are you?" Wilde demanded.

"FBI Special Agents Mack Hunter and Anna Rivers. Carter Wilde and Dr. Joel McCabe, you are under arrest," Mack said.

"Sorry, agent but you don't have jurisdiction here," Wilde said. "In fact, you might say you just walked into a shit storm." Wilde turned and waved his arm.

The four Cryptos appeared and pointed their submachine guns at the two FBI agents.

"I suggest if you have firearms," Wilde said, "take them out slowly, and put them on the ground."

"Can't do that," Mack said but didn't make any attempt to draw his gun.

"The game's up," Anna said. "Tell your boys to drop their weapons."

Wilde let out a boisterous laugh and the two doctors joined in.

Don't these fools see they're clearly outgunned?

"Take their guns," Wilde said. "We'll drop their bodies over the Pacific."

"I hardly think that will be necessary," a woman's voice said.

Wilde turned and saw an Asian woman entering the hangar. "Jesus, and who the hell are you?" Two of the Cryptos trained their weapons on the new arrival.

"My name is Li Jing Lee with Interpol."

"Come on lady. If you're here to arrest me, forget it. There are no extradition laws in Hangshong Providence. If anyone should know that, it should be *you*."

"Yes, you are right, Mr. Wilde," Li Jing said. "But you see, this particular airfield is not in Hangshong Providence. Therefore, you are no longer protected." And with that, Li Jing blew a whistle.

Fifty Interpol police officers stormed the hangar, each wearing a bulletproof vest and tactical gear, and brandishing a compact automatic rifle. Seeing that they were obviously outnumbered, the Cryptos dropped their weapons without a fight.

Mack took out his handcuffs and walked up to Carter Wilde. "Hands behind your back."

"On what charges?" Wilde said skeptically.

"Oh, let's see," Mack said. "Smuggling, gunrunning, aiding and abetting a known criminal, kidnapping, stolen goods, attempted murder..."

"Attempted murder?"

"Yeah, we just got the call. Henry Chang is pressing charges."

"That's a lie. I never tried to kill him. I even told my man..."

"Told your man what?" Mack said.

"Never mind. You're wasting your time," Wilde said as Mack cinched on the bracelets. "My lawyers will have me out within the hour."

"We'll see about that," Anna said. She stepped over to Dr. McCabe and saw his arm was in a sling. "Give me your good hand."

The doctor extended his hand. Anna clamped the handcuff on his wrist, pulled his arm around, and secured the other end to the back of McCabe's belt. "There, that should hold you." She looked over at Li Jing. "Your turn."

Interpol Agent Lee walked over to Dr. Zhang. "Dr. Haun Zhang you are under arrest for the murder of Rong Tran and the murders of five of your students from University."

"This is absurd. You will never—"

"Save it for the magistrate," Li Jing said, cutting him off. She turned to the police officers closest to her and said, "Take them away."

While Wilde, McCabe, and Zhang were being escorted out of the hangar, Mack and Anna hung back to speak with Li Jing.

"What do you think?" Anna asked the Interpol agent.

"I cannot say for Wilde and McCabe," Li Jing said, "but Dr. Zhang will be going to prison for a very long time."

"I don't know about you two, but I could really use a drink," Anna said.

"How about Hangshong mango margaritas?" Li Jing said. "My treat."

50

NOAH'S ARK

Lucas Finder was surprised Luan Chang wanted him to assist her in the rescue effort at the remote airfield, especially after his boss had abandoned Luan's father and left him for dead. Maybe things would have been different if Henry Chang had actually died, but he hadn't. Chang was being treated at a temporary military medical shelter, one of hundreds being set up in the province to treat the tens of thousands injured from the earthquake.

Gas generators powered the spotlights positioned within the interior and the outside of the hangar. A platoon of soldiers guarded the area cordoned off with endless ribbons of yellow crime scene barrier tape.

As there was no location to transport the planeload of animals that had not been affected by the earthquake, makeshift containments and habitats were being erected by the animal keepers along the inside perimeter of the warehouse-sized hangar, all directed by Song Li and Lyle Mason. Those creatures small enough were kept in their cages.

A cacophony of animal cries echoed in the cavernous building.

Finder stood next to Luan and watched the workers offloading the cages from the cargo plane. In some cases, there were two of the same creatures in a single cage. "This is quite the menagerie," Finder said.

And it was.

Dr. Zhang had managed to clone his creations and Luan's as well.

"Or should I say Noah's Ark." Finder glanced around at the different cages and saw a pair of white Fuzhu fawns, some one-eyed Huan kittens, a pair of Lutoulang donkey-headed wolf foal-cubs, four opposing one-armed Yibimin monkeys (in separate cages), a birdcage with Qizhong owl chicks, duos of blue downy-feathered raptors, two Xing-Xing infants, and many more oddities, including two fledgling Xiangliu nine-headed dragons.

"So you had no idea what Dr. Zhang was up to?" Finder said.

"No! I can not believe he could do this right under my nose," Luan said.

And under such a beautiful nose, Finder thought to himself. "As well as your father's. Don't feel bad. I imagine Zhang had quite a bit of help from my boss."

Luan looked at Finder. "Don't you mean...your ex-boss?"

"Yes, of course. First chance I get, I'll make it official. Believe me, I've been wanting to part ways with Carter Wilde for a very long time."

"I hope you will stay," Luan said.

"What would I do?"

"Were you not the construction manager for Wilde Enterprises?"

"Yes, before I became Chief Operating Officer."

"You could help rebuild our city," Luan said.

"Is that the only reason you want me to stay?"

"Well, no," Luan said with a smile.

"What about these creatures?" Finder asked. "What will happen to them?"

"They will remain here where they will be safe for now," Luan said.

"And Cryptid Kingdom?" Finder asked.

"Perhaps, when the time is right," Luan paused for a moment to reflect then gazed out at the cages staged along the hangar wall, "we will try again."

51

WELCOME HOME

While Jack and Nora had been away, their close friend Miguel Walla had finished retrofitting their barn into a DIY workspace for Jack and ample living quarters for Lennie. Miguel had subdivided the lower floor in equal sized sections.

Jack's with a workbench and cabinets to hold his tools, an open area large enough to park half a dozen vehicles if need be.

Lennie's room a sprawling stall with straw strewn on the dirt floor and hamper-sized wicker baskets that Nora could keep stocked with fruit and other edibles whenever Lennie chose not to forage in the woods.

There was also the hayloft on the upper floor with a view of the trees through the window once used for hoisting in bales of hay. The vaulted space designated to be Nora's office.

But now the barn had a different purpose: a place of celebration.

Friends from around the rural town of Rocklin Falls were in attendance.

Sheriff Abe Stone and his wife, Clare, brought freshly baked bread; Myrtle Cooper, tubs of her county fair award-winning goat cheese processed from Clare's dairy goats; Maria Walla, Miguel's wife, handmade tamales and refried beans enough to feed a small army.

Jack stood in front of the barbeque pit a few yards from the barn entrance and was in charge of grilling hamburgers and steaks; Miguel tasked with keeping the ice chests filled with beer and soft drinks; Nora's job to bake a cake.

Sophia, Miguel and Maria's 9-year-old daughter, was having fun, throwing a stick for the family's black Labrador, Rosie to retrieve.

Rounder, the Stone's Pyreneans that shepherded Clare's flock of goats, chose to lie under a shade tree and watch the girl and her dog play. The smell of grilled meat wafted in the air. Rounder lifted his head and salivated, thick drool dripping from his jowls.

"Need a hand there?" Miguel asked, joining Jack and giving his friend a bottle of beer.

"Thanks," Jack said, accepting the beer and taking a swig. "No, I think I got it covered. I have to say, Nora and I are quite impressed. The barn looks great."

"It's the least I could do after what you and Nora went through."

Jack heard a car engine and saw a blue Honda Civic pull up and park with the other guests' vehicles. Gabe and Caroline got out and walked up the driveway.

"Hi everyone," Gabe said.

"Hey, you made it," Jack said and looked at his friend. "Miguel, you remember Gabe?"

"Sure do," Miguel said and shook Gabe's hand. "Cryptid Zoo. You were with your family."

"That's right," Gabe replied. He glanced at Caroline. "This is my girlfriend, Caroline Rollins."

"Caroline is Senator Jonathan Rollin's daughter," Jack told Miguel. "The senator was the one that secured a transport plane from the Air force so we could all fly back with Lennie."

"Good to have connections in high places," Miguel said.

"You got that right." Jack turned and looked at the wide banner stretched across the rafters just inside the barn: WELCOME HOME LENNIE

"You think he even knows why we're all here?" Miguel asked.

"I doubt it," Jack replied, flipping over a succulent strip of London broil. "It's the thought I guess."

"Where is the brute, by the way?"

"He's around somewhere." Jack glanced in the barn at the three long picnic tables covered with checkered tablecloths and party decorations, formed into a T-shape so everyone could see each other seated on the benches.

The screen door banged open against the rear of the house. Nora came down the steps slowly, trying her best not to drop the cake on a large plate.

"Let me help you with that," Miguel called out. He put his beer bottle down and rushed over to Nora. He reached out and took the cake.

"Thank you, Miguel," Nora said.

"No problem," he smiled. Miguel walked the cake over to Jack.

Jack studied Nora's cake; knowing baking was not one of her strong suits. The icing needed to be smoothed out and the shape of the cake was more of an oblong than a rectangle. Nora had spelled out WE LOVE YOU LENNIE in squiggly letters with three different colored icings, and drawn—as though she might have done it with her eyes closed—a childlike caricature of a Yeren's face with M&M eyes and a chocolate sprinkles grin.

Nora smiled at Gabe and Caroline. "I'm so glad you were able to come." She gave them both a warm hug. "Please, help yourself to something in the cooler."

"Thanks," Gabe said. He grabbed a couple soft drinks and gave Caroline a can.

"What do you think?" Nora said, referring to her cake. She reached into the cooler for a pony of wine.

"Looks...tasty," Jack replied.

"I worked hard on that."

"I bet you did."

"I'll go put it on the table," Miguel said. Gabe and Caroline followed him into the barn. Miguel came out a few seconds later.

"I was telling Miguel how impressed we are with the work he did on the barn," Jack said to Nora.

"Yes, thank you so much, Miguel," Nora said. "It really does look beautiful."

"I'm glad you like it," Miguel said. "You know if you ever—"

Someone yelled—maybe Clare, maybe Myrtle—"Oh God, look what he's done," and then everyone inside the barn broke out laughing.

"What the heck?" Jack said. He rushed into the barn, Miguel and Nora right on his heels.

"Looks like someone likes cake," Abe said, laughing along with the others.

"Lennie!" Nora shouted when she saw the cake was no longer on the plate.

The twelve-foot tall Yeren couldn't disguise his guilty look, even behind a face covered with frosting and fudge filling.

Jack, Miguel, and Nora joined in the merriment.

"Leave it to Lennie to crash his own party," Jack said.

TO THE READER

I hope you enjoyed *CRYPTID KINGDOM*. To the best of my knowledge Hangshong Province in China is a figment of my imagination and does not really exist. When I wrote *Cryptid Zoo*, I hadn't planned that it would become a series; and here we are—*Cryptid Kingdom* (*Cryptid Zoo Book 6*). If you liked the series, you can learn more about these characters in *CRYPTID ISLAND*, the exciting prequel to *CRYPTID ZOO* and its sequel *CRYPTID COUNTRY* followed by *CRYPTID CIRCUS, CRYPTID NATION* and of course this installment *CRYPTID KINGDOM* and coming out soon by Severed Press *CRYPTID FRONTIER*.

ACKNOWLEDGEMENTS

I would like to thank Gary Lucas, Romana Baotic, Nichola Meaburn, and the wonderful people working with Severed Press that helped with this book. It's truly amazing how folks who live in the most incredible places in the world can truly enrich our lives. A special thanks to my wonderful daughter and faithful beta reader, Genene Griffiths Ortiz, for her enthusiasm and making this so much fun. And of course, I would like to thank you, the reader, for taking the time to share these bizarre and incredible journeys with me.

ABOUT THE AUTHOR

Gerry Griffiths lives in San Jose, California, with his wife and their five rescue dogs and a cat. He is a Horror Writers Association member and has over thirty published short stories in various anthologies and magazines, along with a collection entitled *Creatures* and his latest novel *In Case of Carnage: A Paranormal Crime Novel.* He is also the author of *Silurid, The Beasts of Stoneclad Mountain, Death Crawlers, Deep in the Jungle, The Next World, Battleground Earth, Down From Beast Mountain, Terror Mountain, Cryptid Zoo, Cryptid Country, Cryptid Island, Cryptid Circus, Cryptid Nation* and *Cryptid Kingdom.*

CHECK OUT OTHER GREAT BIGFOOT NOVELS

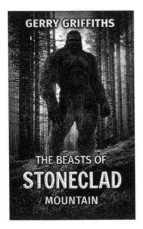

THE BEASTS OF STONECLAD MOUNTAIN
by **Gerry Griffiths**

Clay Morgan is overjoyed when he is offered a place to live in a remote wilderness at the base of a notorious mountain. Locals say there are Bigfoot living high up in the dense mountainous forest. Clay is skeptic at first and thinks it's nothing more than tall tales.

But soon Clay becomes a believer when giant creatures invade his new home and snatch his baby boy, Casey.

Now, Clay and his wife, Mia, must rescue their son with the help of Clay's uncle and his dog, a journey up the foreboding mountain that will take them into an unimaginable world...straight into hell!

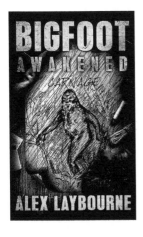

BIGFOOT AWAKENED
by **Alex Laybourne**

A weekend away with friends was supposed to be fun. One last chance for Jamie to blow off some steam before she leaves for college, but when the group make a wrong turn, fun is the last thing they find.

From the moment they pass through a small rural town they are being hunted by whatever abominations live in the woods.

Yet, as the beasts attack and the truth is revealed, they learn that despite everything, man still remains the most terrifying evil of them all.

CHECK OUT OTHER GREAT CRYPTID NOVELS

SWAMP MONSTER MASSACRE
by **Hunter Shea**

The swamp belongs to them. Humans are only prey. Deep in the overgrown swamps of Florida, where humans rarely dare to enter, lives a race of creatures long thought to be only the stuff of legend. They walk upright but are stronger, taller and more brutal than any man. And when a small boat of tourists, held captive by a fleeing criminal, accidentally kills one of the swamp dwellers' young, the creatures are filled with a terrifyingly human emotion—a merciless lust for vengeance that will paint the trees red with blood.

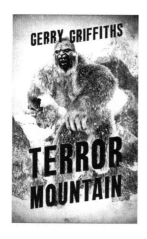

TERROR MOUNTAIN
by **Gerry Griffiths**

When Marcus Pike inherits his grandfather's farm and moves his family out to the country, he has no idea there's an unholy terror running rampant about the mountainous farming community. Sheriff Avery Anderson has seen the heinous carnage and the mutilated bodies. He's also seen the giant footprints left in the snow—Bigfoot tracks. Meanwhile, Cole Wagner, and his wife, Kate, are prospecting their gold claim farther up the valley, unaware of the impending dangers lurking in the woods as an early winter storm sets in. Soon the snowy countryside will run red with blood on TERROR MOUNTAIN.

CHECK OUT OTHER GREAT CRYPTID NOVELS

RETURN TO DYATLOV PASS
by J.H. Moncrieff

In 1959, nine Russian students set off on a skiing expedition in the Ural Mountains. Their mutilated bodies were discovered weeks later. Their bizarre and unexplained deaths are one of the most enduring true mysteries of our time. Nearly sixty years later, podcast host Nat McPherson ventures into the same mountains with her team, determined to finally solve the mystery of the Dyatlov Pass incident. Her plans are thwarted on the first night, when two trackers from her group are brutally slaughtered. The team's guide, a superstitious man from a neighboring village, blames the killings on yetis, but no one believes him. As members of Nat's team die one by one, she must figure out if there's a murderer in their midst—or something even worse—before history repeats itself and her group becomes another casualty of the infamous Dead Mountain.

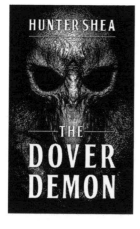

DOVER DEMON
by Hunter Shea

The Dover Demon is real...and it has returned. In 1977, Sam Brogna and his friends came upon a terrifying, alien creature on a deserted country road. What they witnessed was so bizarre, so chilling, they swore their silence. But their lives were changed forever. Decades later, the town of Dover has been hit by a massive blizzard. Sam's son, Nicky, is drawn to search for the infamous cryptid, only to disappear into the bowels of a secret underground lair. The Dover Demon is far deadlier than anyone could have believed. And there are many of them. Can Sam and his reunited friends rescue Nicky and battle a race of creatures so powerful, so sinister, that history itself has been shaped by their secretive presence?

Made in the USA
Middletown, DE
04 March 2023

26209270R00088